Clutch

(Custom Culture, #2)

TESS OLIVER

CLUTCH

Copyright © 2013 by Tess Oliver

ISBN-13: 978-1493701377

ISBN-10: 1493701371

CHAPTER 1

Clutch

The smug little runt sneered at me over the top of his car, and I wanted to pound him into the ground like a tent stake. I'd been racing my sixty-nine Chevelle all spring, but I'd never made it to the final drag. The twerp climbing into his nitrous pumped Chevy SS had won every heat. His head had grown bloated from it, and it definitely needed some deflating.

I ducked down and climbed into the custom front seat that had been lowered to accommodate my height. The car creaked and leaned slightly toward the driver's side. Racing was the only thing that made me regret being so friggin' tall. I was like a massive paperweight in my Chevy. It definitely gave my paperclip sized opponent an advantage.

The crystal blue spring sky had muted with the grays and yellows of sunset. The dry Santa Ana winds were strong enough to tilt the palm trees lining the track and carried enough warmth for the spectators to dress as if it was a summer night. Rowdy, the guy who organized the amateur drag racing events, gave me the signal to head to the staging area, and I fired up the engine.

The four-fifty-four big block roared like a dragon, and I squeezed the steering wheel. "That's right, Sweetheart. Let's show them what you've got."

An impressively large crowd had gathered to watch. Nix's tall head stood out over the other spectators, but I couldn't see Scotlyn. She was, no doubt, attached securely to his arm.

The Christmas tree of lights lit up as I rolled to the starting line. I could see the SS out of the corner of my eye. I really wanted this, and it wasn't just because my opponent was an irritating gnat. Nix always insisted that I was way too hard on myself, that it was all right not to succeed at everything, but that just didn't fly in my world. My rigid determination had helped me earn a hell of a lot of money since high school, and, to me, failure of any kind was out of the question. Dray had insisted my need to win these drag races helped me cope with my lack of girlfriend, or as he had so eloquently put it, 'having no one to fuck.' The asshole had finally found himself in a relationship, and suddenly, he'd become a goddamn expert. Of course, I'd feel pretty cocky too if I had someone as awesome as Cassie. She was definitely the best thing that had ever happened to Dray.

I gripped the steering wheel, and the car vibrated anxiously like a racehorse at the starting gate. I glanced into the rearview mirror. The track beneath my rear wheels was watered. The screeching sound of tires and the acrid smell of melting rubber filled the evening air. The three amber lights winked at me before the tree flashed green and my foot flattened the pedal.

The Chevelle exploded through the cloud of smoke. I could see the flash of yellow paint next to me for a second and then it fell back. My gaze shot up to the rearview mirror as I crossed the line. I would have been pissed as hell if the guy had crashed or blown a tire. I wanted to win this fairly. His car drove up next to mine. I'd won. I waved politely at my opponent. His tires shrieked as he whipped the car around and headed back to the pits.

Cassie emerged from the line of spectators, her camera hanging around her neck. She tapped the window of the car. I cranked it down, and as I looked up at her, she snapped my picture.

She held up her camera and squinted into the screen. The tiny silver hoop in her lip danced as she twisted her mouth in disappointment. "Dammit. I really need to be able to get that fleeting moment of emotion when you win a race. It's gone by the time you stop."

"Well, Cass, unless you can figure out a way to lay across the hood with your camera poised as I cross the finish line, I don't think that's ever going to happen."

Her eyes opened wide as if she was actually considering it. It was hard to get used to her without her glasses but she'd occasionally taken to wearing contacts because of her new found hobby— photography. And she was damn good at it. She could capture the raw emotion and action in one shot that told you an entire story in one frame. Recently, she'd sold a few photos to magazines, and it seemed her talent only grew with each shot.

"You can't strap yourself to my hood, if that's what you're thinking, Cass. Maybe I could just try and recreate the look."

"Nah, it wouldn't be real."

"Well, if you want to capture that *agony of defeat* moment, I'm pretty sure my opponent is still wearing it."

She laughed. "I did hear some rather unsavory language

coming from his car as he sped past." She looked back toward the spectators. "I'll climb back through the crowd and find Nix and Scottie. I don't know if Dray made it or not. He texted me that there was a shitload of traffic on the freeway."

"I'll see you guys in a minute. We'll have to go back to my place for some pizza and beer. I'm in the mood to celebrate." I whipped the car around and waved to the line of onlookers who cheered as I rolled past.

My opponent was already in the pits cursing out some dumbfounded-looking stooge who must have been acting as his mechanic. The guy was as shitty a loser as he was a winner He was definitely the kind of jerk who would blame the mechanic for his loss.

Nix and Scotlyn turned heads as they made their way through the crowd. Even in jeans and sweatshirts, they looked as if they'd just walked out of a fashion magazine. Cassie scurried up behind them, her attention caught by something in her camera viewer. She was short and petite, and the big camera around her neck looked heavy enough to pull her over. Her love for photography rivaled my passion for cars, and lately, I'd noticed Dray was slightly jealous of her newfound hobby. Mostly because it drew attention away from him. The three made their way through the mass of people milling about. They reached me as I climbed out of the driver's seat.

Nix held out his fist. "Nailed it."

"Damn right. I knew the Chevelle could beat that blowhard in his laughing gas amped rust pile. Just needed the right circumstances." I looked at Scotlyn and smiled. "You can release that death grip on his arm, Scottie. The race is over."

A pink blush covered her cheeks, and she loosened her grip on Nix's arm. I teased her way too much when she came to the races. They made her nervous as hell—and with good reason. No one would be able to survive the horrors of a deadly car accident and not have a freak-out session when two cars hurtled down a slick track at top speed.

"Congratulations, *Boss*," she said quietly. Most of us had only had the pleasure of hearing her soft, breathy voice for a few months, and even now, she was noticeably quiet when she was stressed or upset about something. Everything about Scotlyn was still so frighteningly vulnerable, it seemed that anything unexpected could send her newly found voice back into the black hole of anguish that had once swallowed it. But as vulnerable as Scotlyn seemed, my best buddy, Nix, the guy who had always reeked confidence, even annoyingly so, when it came to girls, looked so completely susceptible to heartbreak now that it showed up in every one of Cassie's pictures. Scotlyn was his and that was more than clear, but it was also painfully clear that if Nix ever lost her, he would be shattered beyond repair. It was still hard for me to fathom that the Heartbreak Kid had given away his heart, but Scotlyn was really something. My two best friends had found amazing women. I had girls too, but they were dressed in shiny chrome and had expensive drinking habits— gasoline. I had money and plenty of friends but lately I'd felt my life was seriously lacking. In my quest to focus on business and success, I'd completely ignored my heart.

Dray came up behind me. "Dude, I missed the whole fucking thing. Damn traffic." The ugly deep gash next to his eye, a souvenir from his last fight, had almost healed but it was going to leave a gnarly scar. He dropped his arm around Cassie's shoulder, but she shrugged it off.

"You smell like Long Beach harbor," she complained.

Dray grinned. "Oh come on, you know it turns you on." He looked back at me. "Can you do it again?"

"Sorry, my sport doesn't work like that. One shot is all you've got. And there's no tapping out either."

Dray laughed. "Sport? What sport? All you do is sit in your car and drive a straight line for a quarter mile. I need more skill to take a crap."

Cassie smacked him on the arm and then winced as she rubbed her hand. "God, do you have to bring up gross stuff like that all the time?" Cassie was crazy about the guy, but sometimes the fact that they were polar opposites was awkwardly obvious.

Dray held up his hands. "What do you want from me? I work in the shipyard all day. What do you think we talk about? Baking cookies?"

Cassie tilted her head in annoyance. "So you're all out there cruising around on your forklifts and talking about bowel movements?"

He shrugged. "The topic comes up occasionally." Dray opened his mouth to continue, but Cassie pressed her small hand against his mouth.

"Just shut up."

Dray fell silent. There was nothing more awesome than knowing that my tough, wiry friend, who could lay out a guy twice his size with one punch, could be rendered completely defenseless by a hundred pound girl with coke bottle glasses and an addiction to cheesy romance novels.

I patted the hood of my car like a cowboy patting his horse's neck. "Well, I'm pumped about winning. Meet at my house for pizza and beer. I'm buying."

***

The winds had softened and a perfect, warm California night had fallen over the city. I pulled into my driveway. The bent up Pontiac that I'd put so much time and money into stared sadly back at me. I needed to break it down for parts, but I hadn't had the stomach to do it yet. I'd planned on selling it for big bucks, but Taylor had driven off in it and totaled it. That impulsive decision had earned her a trip to an aunt's house in Florida for her last year of high school. Her parents and her brother, my business partner, had decided she was too out of control, but it seemed to me they'd just wanted her out of their hair. I hadn't gone to see her off, and the guilt of it still pained me. I had steeled myself against my feelings for Taylor so often that it had been easy to pretend I'd agreed with her parents. I was sure she hated me for it. But I knew damn well that I hadn't gone with her to the airport because I couldn't bear to say good bye.

The pizza parlor was on speed dial, along with every other good food place within a twenty mile radius. I pressed the phone to my ear and headed to the door. My mind was on pepperoni and onions and I hadn't noticed the motorcycle until I nearly fell over it. I looked up toward the house but the front stoop was empty.

I stared down at the bike as I finished my pizza order. Nix and Dray pulled up to the curb. Dray and Cassie came up the driveway first.

"Whose bike?" Dray asked.

I shrugged. "I'm not sure. It's in bad shape. Maybe someone wants it restored." I glanced around. "Kind of strange for them to just drop it off without a note."

Dray slapped me on the shoulder. "Well, solve the mystery later. I'm starved. When is the pizza coming?"

"Forty-five minutes but I've got some chips and beer in the kitchen." Dray, Cassie and I headed up the front porch steps as Nix and Scotlyn came up the driveway. Nix spotted the bike right away. "I thought you hated working on bikes."

"It's not mine. I don't know where it came from," I called to him as I stuck the key in the door.

"It looks like a beat up version of that bike your brother used to ride." Dray's comment hit me like a slap on the back.

"Shit." I shoved open the door and stepped inside.

Barrett stood up from the couch, his eyes wide and framed by dark rings. He shoved his hands deep into the pocket of his jeans, but I hadn't missed the tremble in his fingers before he'd hidden them. None of my four brothers were as massively built as me, and at six feet, Barrett had been not only the youngest but the smallest of us all. But the younger brother I remembered had had an impressive, muscular build. When we were teenagers, we had surfed a lot, and when Barrett had walked out of the waves with his board, you could hear a collective gasp coming from the lips of every female on the sand.

"Hey, Jimmy," the wavering sound of it was sadly consistent with his appearance. The guy in front of me looked like a gray, misty shadow of my brother. His long blond hair hung to his shoulders in greasy tangles. Barrett had always been like Nix, admired, good looking and charming, and just like my best friend, my brother could knock a room silent just by entering it. At this moment, he had certainly knocked my friends mute, but the shocked silence was not from awe. Barrett looked like shit. My kid brother was strung out.

Our dad had worked three jobs to keep us in shoes, shelter and food, but he'd hardly ever had time for us. Mom had spent her days keeping house and cooking meals. Being the youngest, Barrett had had the least parental attention of any of us. But he'd caught our dad's attention and ire when he'd gotten expelled from high school for drug possession. Dad had called in a favor from an old navy buddy who owned a crab fishing boat up in Alaska. "Hard work, brutal weather and long hours will keep you out of mischief," Dad had said as he handed Barrett a hundred dollars and a pair of tall rubber boots.

"What the hell, Rett? What's happened? I thought you were out on the Bering Sea?"

He shrugged nonchalantly, but he seemed ready to jump out of his skin. "Yeah, there's a funny story behind that." He looked around at the familiar and unfamiliar faces. "Hey Nix, hey Dray." It seemed to take all his energy to speak.

"Good to see you, Rett," Nix said quietly.

"Hey, Buddy, missed ya." There was a slight hitch in Dray's tone, a hesitation I'd never heard before. Even though Barrett had been almost three years younger than us, he'd hung out with us a lot. He and Dray had always managed to get into trouble together, and they'd grown close because of it.

An awkward silence followed, and Barrett fidgeted like

a nervous kid standing in front of class.

"You know, Clutch, I think we're going to head out," Nix said suddenly. "We've both got to be up early for work."

"Yeah, us too," Dray said.

My evening of celebration had come to a bad end, and as much as I loved my friends, I was anxious for them to leave. And being good friends, they'd obviously sensed it. "Thanks for watching the race. See you at work tomorrow, Scotlyn." I walked out onto the porch with them, out of earshot of Barrett.

Nix turned back to me. "He looks really bad. Call if you need us."

Scotlyn stepped toward me and placed her hand on my arm. Her round blue eyes were shiny with tears. "Ibuprofen, hot baths when the chills get bad, and don't expect him to sleep much. And try not to be too hard on him. I assure you, he's already being punished."

"Thanks." I watched them walk down the driveway and took a deep breath before returning to the house.

Barrett leaned up against the door jamb for support.

I stood speechless for a second, still in shock from his withered appearance. "When was the last time you ate?" I asked finally.

He pulled one hand from its restraining pocket and combed his long hair back off his face with shaky fingers. "It's been a few days."

"Christ, Rett, a few *days*?" I had to consciously squash the anger in my tone. Scotlyn was right. It was the last thing he needed at the moment. "I've got pizza coming."

His face paled at the mention of pizza, and he shook his

head. "Don't think I can keep anything down yet." The agony in his voice felt like a sledgehammer against my chest.

"Let me get you to a hospital."

The suggestion startled him, and he pushed off the doorjamb. I lunged forward and caught him before he collapsed to the ground. My arms went around him, and his shoulders shook. "No hospitals, Jimmy." The words cracked out of his throat. "Please, let me stay here. I'll be out of your way soon, I promise." His last words shot out on a sob. I hadn't seen or heard my brother cry since he was twelve and our dog had gotten hit by a car, and the sound of it felt as if a cold, wet shadow had covered me.

I could no longer support his weight. I held him tightly as we fell. He shuddered uncontrollably in my arms, and I tightened my hold on him, foolishly thinking that somehow I could stop the trembling and the pain. "Goddammit, Rett, what the hell have you done?" I muttered quietly. "What the fucking hell have you done?"

Chapter 2

Clutch

I poured myself a third cup of coffee and replaced the pot on the coffee maker with care. It seemed even the slightest disturbance of air could wake Barrett. It had been a three day long journey into hell, and my kid brother had spent half of it draped over the toilet and the other half like a human burrito, rolled up tightly in two thick blankets. He had dozed off occasionally but would wake with a start, groaning with every movement.

When he was little, I'd taken care of him whenever he'd gotten hurt, and wild kid that he was, it had happened a lot. We'd once taken a steep road on our skateboards and Barrett had hit a rock and lost control . . . along with a good amount of skin. I'd carried him, miserable and bloodied, all the way home on my back. But this time there was nothing I could do for him. For three nights in a row, I'd stretched out in the bed next to Rett, jolting with my own mental pain every time he writhed and twisted in physical pain. It was like watching someone being tortured slowly and with increasing intensity until death was not just welcome but prayed for.

I'd never stayed away from the shop for more than half a day, but Scotlyn had assured me she had everything under control. I'd told Jason that I had to drive out of the state to pick up some parts. I hadn't been ready to tell him anything about Barrett yet. Jason was a close friend and business partner but he tended to be far more judgmental than Nix and Dray. Although, if they hadn't seen it first hand, I might not have told them either. It was one of those family problems better left under wraps.

After three long days and nights, fatigue and lack of sleep had taken a toll on both of us. Things had gotten rough the night before. Barrett had hurled the bottle of Ibuprofen at the wall and begged me to hold a pillow over his face and I'd almost been tempted to take him up on it. By midnight we'd finally been pushed to our physical and mental limits. I'd poured two shots of whiskey down his throat. He'd gagged on the bitterness of it but it seemed to have taken the edge off . . . at least for a few hours.

I needed to take some parts into the shop and check on a few orders and then I would head back home. Barrett would be on his own for a few hours, and with any luck, he'd sleep through my absence.

I downed the last cup of strong coffee, but it did nothing to clear the grogginess from my head. I would have to blast my stereo just to stay awake during the commute to the shop. In my state of exhaustion, I'd forgotten that I'd tiptoed around all morning to not wake my brother. I scooted back and the chair scraped the tile floor. The grating sound echoed through the house. I froze and listened to see if my carelessness had woken Barrett. The house remained still. I stood and walked silently, a nearly impossible task with size fourteen boots and wood floors, to the living room for my keys.

A small moan rolled up from the hallway, and Barrett stepped into the living room, looking less like the guy that all the girls in high school had drooled over and more like one of the zombies from Day of the Dead. The two blankets seemed to be weighing down his shoulders and standing took all his strength. His arm lifted and he held up a crumpled piece of paper.

"What's that?" I asked.

"Please, Jimmy, you've got to help me. I'm not going to survive this. I just need something to hold me over for a few more days. This guy lives near—"

I snatched the paper from his hand and tore it up. He stared down at the pieces as if I'd torn up a piece of his soul. Then, moving with speed that I would not have thought him capable of, he lunged at me with his fist. I threw up a hand and his knuckles smacked my palm hard. He grabbed his arm and dropped to his knees. "Just fucking kill me, Jimmy. Break my neck or something. Just put me out of my misery."

I yanked him to his feet, and for a second, I saw that blue eyed, cocky little fucker who, growing up, had followed me around like an annoying pest, an annoying pest who everyone loved. Barrett could win people over with a gesture as simple as a smile or handshake, and now he stood in front of me looking like the worst the human race had to offer. I felt his despair as if it flowed from him into my hands. I helped him to the couch and tucked the blankets in tightly around him.

"Are you ready for some food?"

With the blanket tucked below his chin, he peered up at me like a scared kid who had just been woken by a horrible nightmare. Unfortunately, this bad dream was all too real. "Not unless it contains poison."

"Right, you wish I'd let you off that easily." I straightened and stared down at him. "You're going to suffer every moment of this, lil' bro. Maybe it will help remind you to never do it again."

He moved his head side to side weakly. I hated seeing defeat on Barrett's face. The only other time I'd seen it was when Dad had told him he was going to Alaska. The look had never suited him, and it was even harder to see now. "Doesn't work that way, Jimmy. You forget pain after it's gone. Otherwise there wouldn't be any second babies born in the world."

"That's a stupid fucking analogy. Women are rewarded for the pain of birth with a baby."

He closed his eyes. "You're right. This pain has no reward at the end," his voice trailed off, and it seemed he'd fallen asleep again. His cheeks were pale and sunken as a quiet snore rolled up from his throat.

"Yes there is, Rett. You get your life back." I walked to the front door and looked back at him. The contortions in his face had disappeared and he was relaxed. For a second, he looked like my popular, charming brother again.

I closed the door behind me. We'd kept the blinds closed for the past days and the bright sun stung my tired eyes. I got in the car and leaned over to the glove box for my sunglasses. Bleary headed and feeling as if I'd just run a fucking marathon, I headed to the shop.

***

Scotlyn looked up from the computer monitor. During her years of silence, she'd perfected the art of speaking with facial expressions and her incredible face was easy to read this morning.

"He's had a really awful few nights," I said. "But I think we can get through this." I could hear Jason moving boxes in the back room. "Did you mention anything to Jason yet?"

"Didn't think it was my business," she said softly.

"Thanks. Jason knows my little brother is a handful of trouble." I smiled and thought instantly about Jason's little sister, another package of trouble. "I'll let him know soon. I'm going to head back home this morning. I need to be there. I brought in that intake manifold that the guy with the Nova was looking for. He'll be in here around ten."

"I'll take care of it," Scotlyn said. "You definitely need to be home. Keep him hydrated. That's one of the worst parts about it." She spoke with the confidence of someone who had been through the same nightmare. I hadn't heard all the details of her past, but Nix had told me that the rich asshole, Hammond, had pulled her from the streets where she'd spent some hellish years as a homeless teen. Looking at the stunning, fresh-faced beauty standing across the counter from me, it was nearly impossible to imagine that she had ever lived a gritty life. But that was all behind her now. Hammond was behind bars and out of her life too.

"I went out last night and bought some of that electrolyte stuff. It seemed to make him feel better."

Jason walked out from the back with two boxes. "Dude, it's about time you got here. I heard you won the other night." He stopped and stared at me. "And from the looks of it, you spent just a little too much time celebrating."

"Yeah, in fact I'm not feeling that great. I brought in that intake manifold. I've got some paperwork and then I'm going back home."

Jason smiled and shook his head. "Man, I wish I'd made it to your victory party. Sarah wasn't in the mood to go out the night of your race."

Sarah was never in the mood to do anything, and ever since Jason had moved in with his longtime girlfriend, he'd been under her house rules. He'd had no reason to jump into a commitment with her. Like Taylor, he'd been blessed with the Flinn good looks. He'd had plenty of girls after him, but for some unexplained reason, he'd settled for a woman who seemed to spend all her waking hours figuring out how to control him. He'd grown up under very controlling parents and it would seem logical that he'd avoid living under someone else's iron fist. But strangely enough, he'd slipped happily beneath Sarah's.

"I'll be in the office if you need me." My head felt light from the lack of sleep and hunger. The only food in the house had been the four pizzas that'd come for the celebration that never happened. I managed to finish off one by picking at it one slice at a time, but Barrett's nausea had done a number on my normally ravenous appetite.

I had three orders for rare parts, and I needed to search every corner of the internet for them, but I was sure that staring at a monitor for longer than ten minutes would send me off into a deep sleep. I pulled up my account books, but after five minutes, the numbers were a blur. I rubbed my eyes. My mind kept drifting back to Barrett. I'd thought about calling my parents for all of about two seconds. They were getting on in years, and they would have no comprehension of what Barrett was going through. And, sadly, they would probably just be pissed at him for disgracing the family.

I could only hope that Dad's friend hadn't called to let him know that Barrett had been fired. Dad had spent too many hours watching cable television where the deadly job of crab fishing had been romanticized, leading him to his asinine decision for a punishment that was far too severe for the crime. But Barrett had always been a danger junkie, and even though he had protested his sentence, he'd gone without too much of a fight. When I got home, and if he was capable of answering questions, I planned to grill my brother on exactly what had gone down out there on the fishing boat.

Jason popped his head into my office. "Hey, I just shipped off those El Camino back up lights." He stepped inside. "You look like crap. Get out of here. Scottie and I can handle things today."

My chair creaked as I slumped back against it. Jason was my partner and good friend. I had no real reason except pride to keep anything from him. "Barrett showed up at my house three nights ago."

Jason's eyes rounded. "Thought he was crab fishing."

"So did I." I thought about the shivering, underweight guy I'd left back on my couch and my throat tightened. "He's a mess." Saying it out loud hurt more than I'd expected.

"I'm sorry to hear that, Clutch. I'm sure you'll take good care of him. And Barrett has always been tough." He smiled. "Man, did that guy have the chicks dragging at his heels. Always envied the little twerp for that." He turned to leave but then stopped. "Go home to him." His phone buzzed and he plucked it out of his pocket and looked at it. He laughed. "Speaking of pesky younger siblings." He

19

walked over with his phone. He definitely had my attention.

It was a picture of a Pink's hot dog. I was amazed at how profoundly disappointed I was that the picture wasn't of Taylor.

"She knows how much I love those hot dogs." Jason turned to leave and then he hesitated and his shoulders tensed. He realized his mistake just as it occurred to me that he'd made one. And I'd been worried about keeping secrets from him.

I sat forward. "I didn't know there was a Pink's in Florida."

He hadn't turned back to look at me yet. Apparently, he was trying to formulate a decent excuse for keeping something pretty fucking major from me. And now I wondered why.

He finally had the guts to face me. "Listen, Bro, I was going to tell you." He only called me Bro when he knew I was pissed off about something, and it was obvious from his expression that I was about to get really pissed. "She came back three months ago for her eighteenth birthday and begged my parents to let her stay. She's matured some and my parents agreed, but . . ."

"But what?" This was the last thing I needed after the last few nights I'd had, but now that it was out, I needed to hear the rest of it.

Jason looked down at the ground. "She had to promise to stay away from you."

I leaned forward, resting my forearms on my thighs. I was tired and in a bad mood and his statement felt like a hot poker through my gut. I wasn't completely sure of his parents reasoning behind it, and I wasn't completely sure I wanted to know.

"Look, Jimmy, it's not about you. They like you."

I snorted a derisive laugh and slouched back against the chair. "Well, that's fucking obvious. I mean, what better way to prove it than to forbid their daughter from coming near me."

"It was just that Taylor was so friggin' nuts about you."

I flinched at his words and had no idea why hearing them was so painful.

"Don't you see, Bro? Everything she did, she did to get your attention. She was out of control, and her crush on you only fed her impulsiveness. She's dating a guy her own age now. It has really helped settle her down. "

"I assure you the wild Taylor is still alive and kicking deep inside." After saying it, I realized how much I wanted it to be true. Taylor's spirit was not the kind that should be extinguished or constrained. "She's just afraid she'll be shipped off to another relative." Jason's words had hit me like pieces of shrapnel. All I could think was that the whole thing was beyond messed up. I stared at him. "Did you speak up to defend me at all, or were you right on board with this bullshit?"

His silence said it all. The chair scraped the floor as I stood abruptly. "I'm outta here." I pushed past him. "Thanks a lot, *Bro*."

CHAPTER 3

Taylor

Fortunately, not many people had cravings for a chili dog in the morning, so the lunch crowd hadn't carpeted the sidewalk in front of Pink's yet. Adam had insisted that he needed to get back by fourth period. As it was, it had taken some major begging and a quick make-out session behind the gym before he'd agreed to skip second period. The whole thing made me laugh. My parents were pleased that Adam was such a good influence on me, but most of the time, the complete opposite was true. I was a bad influence on Adam. Or at least I tried.

Adam glanced back over his shoulder and flashed his toothpaste commercial smile at me from the order window. I leaned against the parking meter jutting up from the sidewalk and watched him. Great hair, broad shoulders and a tight butt— the boy had no flaws except for the obvious one— he was a boy. Even though we were both eighteen and seniors, the hierarchy of high school crushes was hard to ignore. For freshman girls, the world of high school was an endless stream of hot junior and senior guys who left trails of aftershave in the hallway and talked about cars and getting laid. But as each year of high school passed, the tables were cruelly turned, and by the time a girl reached her senior year, all the guys seemed like fresh out of puberty, awkward boys. But for the guys, each year brought a new crop of innocent and untried freshmen females.

Unlike most of my friends, I hadn't spent those under-class years pining for the senior class president or football quarterback. For me, there had been only one crush, and it had been a major one, so major that I felt scarred emotion-ally when I thought about it. By the time I'd turned sixteen, I'd given my heart and soul to my brother's best friend, Clutch. Unfortunately, to him, I was just an irritating pain in the ass, and he'd made it all too clear that he was happy to see me go. It was the one thing that had made it easier to follow my parent's command to stay clear of him. I just had to keep reminding myself that Clutch considered me a well rid of nuisance, an opinion that was no doubt set in stone after I'd totaled his prize Pontiac.

"You don't want onions, do you?" Adam called back to me.

"You're kidding, right? Who eats a chili dog without onions? I want that old sourpuss, Mr. Burke, to smell my breath from the front row of his chemistry class."

"What about taking pity on the guy who plans to kiss you after that chemistry class?"

I held out my arms. "I guess if you want that kiss bad enough, you'll overlook a little onion breath."

Adam shook his head as he turned back to the order win-dow.

A loud rattling motor made the sign above the hot dog stand vibrate. The car had pulled up to the meter I was lean-ing against. I looked back over my shoulder. It was a late sixties Charger with more rust than paint. I recognized the driver as he climbed out of the car. I'd seen him a lot at the classic car events where I used to hang before my parents had added those to the list of things that would get me sent back to my painfully dull aunt with a bingo addiction and a house that smelled like moldy sponges.

His friend climbed out of the passenger side, and my heart sprang to fast forward. I didn't know his name, but in one of my more ridiculous and completely worthless attempts to make Clutch jealous, I'd stupidly climbed into the guy's Mustang. The incident had ended with Clutch's fist in the guy's hood. I'd always figured the guy had been lucky that it'd been his car instead of his face. The creep had nostrils the size of headlights, and his hair was always slicked back like he'd spent hours greasing it.

I looked away and back toward Adam hoping that they would walk right past. My hopes were dashed when two tall shadows loomed over the sidewalk in front of my feet.

"Well, those are a pair of legs I haven't seen in a long time," the Mustang guy said.

The driver circled in front of me. His head was shaved clean and some words that were hard to decipher were scribbled around his neck. Definitely not a Freefall tattoo. "You're that sexy thing that always used to hang out with Mason."

I shrugged.

"That asshole still owes me for the dent he put in my Ford."

I grinned at him. "I've got his number. Why don't you call him and ask for it? I'm sure he'd send a check right off."

His mouth tightened, and amazingly, his nostrils grew even larger. "That's right. I just remembered that you had a smart mouth to go along with those trampy—" He went to touch my bottom lip with his grease stained thumb but I smacked his arm away. There was anger in his laugh.

Adam had been oblivious to the scene behind him until he spun around with our hot dogs in hand. His face dropped when he saw the two rather menacing guys hovering over me. He walked several steps and stopped about ten feet away. He didn't seem eager to come any closer.   "Let's go, Taylor. We've got to get back," Adam called with a layer of fear that even the traffic on La Brea Avenue could not have drowned out.

The guy with the dented Mustang caught hold of my arm before I walked away. Obviously still mad about me slapping his arm, his fingers gripped me angrily. "Why don't you ditch Peter Pan and hang with us, Sweetheart."

Adam took one step but then stopped. I didn't know whether to be majorly disappointed or relieved. The two guys were big and mean enough to hurt him, and I'd been the one to talk Adam into ditching school for hot dogs. The worst part of all was watching Adam's face. His expression of helplessness was being overshadowed by a profound look of shame.

I winced as the guy squeezed my arm tighter, and Adam took a cautious step. The driver laughed, showcasing teeth that were brown and mottled from drugs. "Why, Max, I think the school boy with the hot dogs is getting angry. Maybe we should relieve him of those hot dogs too. I'm hungry." He took a step toward Adam.

"Wait," I said. "Let me text my friends that I won't be back for lunch.

Max laughed. "Looks like she's coming with us, kid."

I lifted my phone and quickly ran my fingers over the keypad. The heartbreak on Adam's face sent a pang of guilt through me, but while I wasn't great in chemistry or English literature, I was fairly skilled at devising clever plans. I motioned the driver closer, and he leered at me as he leaned down.

I lowered my voice so that Adam had no idea what I was saying. "I'm not going anywhere with you two losers," I whispered, " but I did just send a picture of your car to Clutch, and I let him know you were bothering me." It was a lie, of course, but I knew bringing up his name would scare the shit out of them. And I was right. Max quickly released my arm.

"Stupid brat. You're not even worth the bother." The driver motioned for his slimy friend to get in the car, and they drove off as if the devil himself had driven them off, a giant, blond devil.

Relief washed over Adam, but it was obvious that his male ego had taken a hit. I decided to act like the whole thing hadn't happened. Adam was one of the most popular guys on campus. He'd recover quickly.

I grabbed my hot dog and snapped a picture to send Jason. "My brother is addicted to these things, but his bitchy girlfriend doesn't like him to eat them." Adam didn't respond. We walked to his car in silence.

"What did you tell them that had them so scared?" he finally asked.

So much for ignoring the whole thing. "I told them you had nearly killed a guy in a fist fight because he'd snaked your parking spot."

Adam stared down at me as I took a big bite of my hot

dog. "Shit, they forgot the onions."

"Did you really tell them that?" he asked.

"Yep." I wiped the chili off my lip with my thumb. "Hey, next time, let me order the hot dogs."

CHAPTER 4

Clutch

A few nights before, I'd won a drag race final and everything had been going great. An hour later, everything had turned to shit, and it only seemed to be getting deeper. I was beat and I was glad to get back home even if I had more crap waiting for me there. I could hear the television as I walked up the driveway. I decided that was a good thing. The first few nights, Rett could not have sat still long enough to watch T.V.

The top of his blond head stuck out over the layers of blankets he had wrapped around him as he sat on the couch staring at the screen. "You're back already?" His voice was muffled by the covers.

I stepped in and looked at the television. "I see you found my stash of porn."

"The only thing on was cooking and morning talk shows."

"So, you're feeling better?"

The mass of blankets moved in what I sensed was a noncommittal shrug. "It comes in waves. I still wouldn't turn down a game of Russian Roulette with a fully loaded pistol."

"I might join in that game. At the moment, those odds sound pretty damn good." Halfway home my head had started to pound from lack of food, and even though Jason's ugly little revelation had turned my stomach against me, I needed to eat. I walked into the kitchen. An open pizza box sat on the table and two slices were missing. I picked up a slice. Even three days old it looked good. "I see you were able to get some food down," I called to the living room.

"Yeah," Rett answered, "for about twenty minutes. I'm never going to be able to look at a pineapple again without gagging."

I stared down at the slice of cold pizza with the shriveled pieces of pineapple and then dropped it back into the box. I grabbed the milk out of the fridge and finished off the half gallon milk container before returning to the living room.

Rett's head popped up like a gopher emerging from a burrow of cotton blankets. I sat down next to him and realized the television was on mute.

"No sound?"

"The dialogue didn't seem all that important."

I grabbed the remote and turned it off. "So, what happened, Rett? You know I'm going to have to call Dad and give him some kind of story before his friend calls him."

He scrunched down farther into his cocoon. "I don't know. It started out all right. The work was hard, especially because I was seasick through most of my shifts." He laughed quietly. "Although 'shift' was not really the word to use. Sometimes we were out on deck for thirty-six hours with just enough break time to eat and piss. I would get so tired my body would just start moving on its own, like my brain was no longer telling it what to do."

"Like cruise-control?"

"Yeah, but even dead tired you had to be ready to react or you risked losing a hand or being swept overboard by a wave." His voice sounded weary, almost as if he was reliving one of those endless nights of fishing in his head. "But I didn't mind, and the captain said I was one of the toughest greenhorns he'd had on board in a couple of years." He grew quiet, and for a moment, it seemed he'd dozed off. "It was hard though, Jimmy. Really hard. I'd fall into my bunk so tired and sore that there were times when I would hope for a disaster so the boat would sink. That way I would never have to leave the bunk again. I'd formed a bond with Gus, the captain's son. One day he offered me a couple of pills to keep me awake and make me feel better. They helped . . . a lot. Then we'd get to port and our pockets would be full and we'd spend five days on dry land partying like they were our last days on Earth. And sometimes, it really felt like it. Every day out on the water felt as if it could easily be my last. The drugs just made it easier to bear."

"So you got caught?"

"Sort of. The captain found a stash, but it wasn't mine. It belonged to Gus, but I took the fall for it."

"Christ, Rett, you're always taking the fall. Just like in high school. You were the only one to get expelled, and your three buddies finished senior year without ever thinking about it again."

"I know. I've got to stop being such a sucker. Anyhow, no other captain would take me, so I hopped on a plane and headed home. I landed in Frisco and stopped at an old high school buddy's house. He'd moved up north after graduation. He's the guy who I'd sold the bike to. He still had it, so I bought it back for the ride south. By then I was starting to feel pretty strung out. The ride home was tough. I didn't think I was going to make it." His voice trailed off, and seconds later, a light snoring sound floated up from the blankets.

I snatched a pillow from the couch, dropped it on the floor, and stretched out. I stared up at the ceiling thinking how much I wanted to throttle the kid, and at the same time I wanted to protect him with my life. Within seconds, fatigue cleared my mind and pushed me into a much needed sleep.

***

The sound of a trash can being dragged down the driveway next door woke me. I sat up feeling only slightly more rested than I had in the morning. Rett was standing in front of the window in just his jeans. He looked painfully thin, and there was a recently healed gash across his shoulders.

"Did the chills finally stop?" I scrubbed my hair with my fingers as I sat up and cracked my back and neck. I pushed to my feet and walked over to the window.

"For now," he answered without pulling his gaze from the outside.

"What happened to your back? They aren't still tying sailors to the moorings for lashings, are they?"

"That would have been less painful. One of the pots came loose and swung into me. Knocked me off my feet and nearly overboard." He watched as my neighbor, Aimee, dressed in her white pharmacy technician dress, dragged a large trash can down to the street. "That can is too heavy for her." Then he looked over at me. "Afterward the captain told me a chilling story about how he'd seen a guy get decapitated by a loose pot. 'Took his head right off and into the sea.' Strangely enough, he seemed to think the story would make me feel better. It didn't. I figured if I'd been just a few inches shorter, my head would've been swimming with the fishes too." Barrett turned back to the window. Aimee climbed into her junk-pile of a car. It backfired twice before rolling down the short driveway.

"She's cute." He shuffled back to the couch and propped his bare feet up on my coffee table. He'd showered, and with his long hair clean and brushed, he looked much closer to the Barrett I remembered. "I thought you lived next to an elderly couple."

"I did but the husband died last year and the wife went into a retirement home. The kids rented the place out to Aimee and Dustin."

"Dustin?"

"Yeah, biggest asshole on the planet. He treats her like shit." I walked into the kitchen, pulled out a pizza box and returned to the living room.

Rett's face went pale at the sight of it.

"Too bad. I'm going to pass out if I don't eat something. Just look the other way and stop thinking about pineapples."

"Why is this guy such an asshole?" He lifted his head off the back of the couch. "Wait, you have a thing for her, don't you?" Then he pressed his hand against his forehead and dropped his head back as if it was filled with sand. "Fuck, I think this headache is going to be permanent."

"Good. It'll remind you not to do anything so stupid again. And, no, I don't have a thing for her. She's very sweet, and I feel bad for her." I plucked the pieces of sausage off the pizza and dropped them back into the box. "These taste like shit cold. Why are you so interested in her?"

"No reason. She just looked kind of sexy struggling with that big trash can."

I laughed and nearly choked on my food. "You've been watching porn all morning. A picture of Aunt Margaret would probably give you a hard on."

"Fuck off." He threw a pillow at me, and I lifted the pizza slice out of its path. "So you don't think she's cute?"

"Yeah, she's cute. But let's face it, Rett, she's not exactly your type."

He didn't have much strength to protest, but he rolled his face my way without lifting his head from the couch. "I like nice girls, especially when they're wearing sexy little uniform dresses."

"Oh, so this is about the uniform." I picked up another slice of cold pizza. "You've been having one of those nurse fantasies."

His middle finger wavered slightly as he lifted it in the air. "You act like it's impossible for me to be attracted to a *nice* girl. I have dated nice girls, occasionally."

"Like hell you have."

"Well, now that I've faced my own death more than once, I'm planning to change my ways."

I laughed. "Anyway, I know Aimee's husband is an asshole of humongous proportions. One day there was a knock on the door and I opened it. Aimee was standing there with a bloody kitchen towel wrapped around her hand. She looked close to passing out. Dustin had been in the middle of some video game tournament and he'd told her to drive herself to the emergency room. She'd cut it making his dinner. She told me she didn't think she could drive, so I took her. While we were in the waiting room, she told me the whole story about how she'd gotten pregnant in high school and Dustin had married her. Then she lost the baby, but by then, her parents had disowned her and she was on her own. She works two jobs and he sits at home and plays video games. We sat in the emergency room for three hours and the dick never called her once to see if she was all right. I took her home that night, and it took all my will not to walk over to the guy and pinch his ugly fat head right off his neck."

"What an asshole." Rett picked the blankets back up off the floor and draped them over his bare chest. "One minute it feels like I'm in the middle of the Sahara, and the next, I'm back in Alaska. Is there anymore of that funny tasting orange stuff? It seems to help with my body temperature."

"You sound just like Mom when she was going through menopause." I went to the fridge to get the electrolyte drink.

"So how's Taylor?" Rett called from the living room.

His question threw me, and by the time I reached the refrigerator I'd forgotten what I'd come in for. I stared at the mostly empty shelves until the orange fluid caught my eye. I returned to the living room and handed him the container. "How the hell should I know?"

He threw his head back and chugged the stuff like it was a cold beer and then dragged the back of his wrist across his mouth. "Oh come on, that chick followed you around everywhere. She was crazy about you. Do you mean to tell me she finally gave up on you?"

The Taylor topic produced a hard knot in my stomach.

"I guess so." I turned the porn back on to put a quick end to the conversation.

Barrett stared at the side of my face. "Man, I just hit a sore spot."

"Those drugs have fried the few brain cells you had. You don't know what you're talking about." I turned up the volume and fake moans and grunts of pleasure filled the air.

"Right," Rett said and then wisely shut up.

CHAPTER 5

Clutch

Barrett and I had spent the rest of the day just hanging out. He'd felt well enough in the evening to eat, and by that time I was ready to eat a damn brontosaurus. The day off had been so good for me, I'd called into the shop to let Scotlyn know that I'd be working from home for another day. I needed some time to absorb everything, and, besides, I'd been working my ass off for months.

No longer hungry, and feeling much better, Barrett had slept through the morning. I'd spent the first half of the day online searching for parts, and my stomach was beginning to protest from lack of attention. I hadn't been to Freefall in ages, and I decided to head over there and pick up Nix for lunch.

I left Barrett a note. It looked as if he was going to sleep most of the day. It was the best thing for him. He'd be up and back to normal soon and then I would have to worry about keeping him out of trouble.

Cassie was standing at the counter working on the receipt book when I walked in. I could hear the buzz of Nix's guns coming from his back room. Cassie glanced up and pushed her glasses up higher on her nose. "Hey, Clutch," she said without much enthusiasm.

I reached the counter. "What's with the frosty greeting?

You mad about something?"

She smiled and shook her head. "Sorry about that. I'm just a little pissed at Dray. That's all." Right then Dray's loud laugh rocked the back room and she sighed. Her big dark eyes were magnified by the thick lenses. "The idiot is getting my name tattooed across his shoulder."

"And this has you pissed because . . ."

She shut the receipt book. "A tattoo is so permanent. I guess I'm just superstitious, but I think it's tempting fate. What if something happens between us? Then he's stuck with my name on his skin. I just think it's a bad idea."

"I get it." I pointed to the obnoxiously arrogant tattoo of a blank billboard with *your name here* written on it. Nix had warned me against getting it, but I'd insisted, and now full regret had set in. "But, I think even though you two are definitely an odd couple, it was meant to be."

"Yeah, maybe," she said sounding not the slightest bit convinced by my argument. Then her face brightened. "Hey, I got a paying gig from a skater magazine. They sent me out to shoot at a skate competition and they liked my stuff."

"That's amazing, Cass. I'm happy for you. I noticed you had your glasses on again."

"I still have the contacts. I just don't like wearing them." She smiled up at me. "I've been wearing thick glasses since I was three."

"Three? Damn, that's young."

She laughed softly. "I was sitting a foot from the television trying hard to watch my favorite cartoon. My mom walked through the room and said, 'Cassie, don't sit so close or it will hurt your eyes'. I was three. I just figured that everyone else was seeing the same blurry mess that I was seeing. Like a good little girl, I scooted back a few inches. But when she walked back through, I had inched forward again. My mom walked up behind me and started crying." Cassie's tone softened as she seemed to be remembering back to the day. She shook the past from her head. "Anyhow, every time I passed a mirror with the contacts I didn't recognize myself. It was creepy. Like a stranger's reflection was staring back at me. Besides, they are a pain to take care of, and I think my pictures are better when I have my glasses on."

I leaned forward and kissed her forehead. "Well, I think you are a goddess with or without them."

A faint blush crept into her cheeks. "And you, my Viking friend, should be the main character in a romance novel."

I looked toward the back room. "So, is it just Dray and Nix back there?"

Her face fell again as I reminded her of the tattoo. Most girls would have been thrilled with the prospect, but Cassie always had both feet firmly on the ground. "Yeah, you can go back."

Nix looked up from his work. "Hey, how's Barrett doing?"

"He's doing a lot better. He rode all the way down from San Francisco on that shitty bike, and I think he was half-starved and dehydrated . . . among other things. Now I just have to keep him from going back to the stuff, which I think will be more than half the battle." Nix and Dray had seen him that night, and there was no way to sugar coat it. I walked over and looked down at the tattoo.

Dray twisted back and looked up at me. "How does it look?"

"Great, but I don't think Cassie's too thrilled about it."

"Yeah, yeah, I know. Can you fucking believe it? Do you know how many chicks would kill to have their name tattooed on my shoulder?"

Nix rolled his eyes.

I glanced back to the front room. "Well, I would have thought Cassie, and that would have been at least one. But apparently the answer is zero."

Nix lifted the gun off Dray's shoulder and laughed hard.

"Look who's talking," Dray said, "I haven't seen anyone fill their name in on your stupid billboard tattoo yet." He laughed and I knew what was coming next. "Unless you count the time Taylor wrote hers in with a permanent marker."

"For someone who gets his head slammed on the mat a lot, you sure hang on to stupid, meaningless memories," I said.

Nix wiped off Dray's shoulder and admired his handiwork. "You're done. Cassie better not be pissed at me about this. You're taking full blame." He looked up at me. "That reminds me, I found something that I think will work to cover that billboard tattoo. I can do it whenever you have time."

"Great."

Dray pushed off the table and walked to the mirror on the wall. He spun around a few times like a dog chasing his tail until Nix passed him a handheld mirror. "Here, Jackass. Unless you're an owl, it's pretty hard to look at your own shoulder blade."

"Looks good." Dray handed the mirror back to Nix. "I think she'll like it." His confidence was dumbfounding.

"Care to lay odds on that?" I asked.

"Shut up." Dray balled his shirt up in his hand. "At least I admit it when I love someone."

Nix laughed. "Yeah, after about a year of denying it."

"It's called self-control, Pal. You should try it sometime. Girls hate desperation." Dray bowed. "Now, if you'll excuse me, I promised my lady some lunch."

Dray's comment had been obnoxious and cocky, like the man himself, but it had hit home. I'd grown up in a house of brothers and had a father who shunned emotional attachments. When something hurt or bothered you, you kept it to yourself or risked getting teased mercilessly. We never even made much out of holidays or birthdays because too much emotion came with those sentimental traditions. I was a fumbling fool when it came to dealing with my feelings, so most of the time I just ignored them. They got in the way of living.

I looked over at Nix. "Thought you might want to go eat. Barrett was sleeping and I took the day off."

"Sounds good, but do you mind if we pick up Scotlyn? I promised her lunch."

"We could postpone it. I don't want to intrude on your date."

Nix looked up from his task. "It's lunch, not a date, and she'd be thrilled to have you along. She adores you."

"At least someone does," I said under my breath.

"What?"

I shook my head. "Oh nothing. Taylor is back in town."

Nix looked back at me over his shoulder. "Again?"

I sat forward. "What do you mean again?"

My sharp tone made him stop what he was doing and turn around. "Well, I knew she'd come into town a few times to visit. Scotlyn mentioned it. What the hell are you so bent up about? Didn't you know?"

"No, I didn't know, but apparently the rest of the world knew."

Nix seemed to be sorting out what I'd just said and then his expression assured me that he'd figured it out. "Jason didn't tell you?"

"Nope. Apparently, she has been forbidden to go anywhere near me."

"But why?"

"It seems I've been the reason behind all of her wild behavior. How do you like that for being the unsuspecting fall guy?"

"That sucks." He turned back around and finished his clean up. "I'm definitely ready for lunch." As he walked toward me, I realized he looked as tired as I'd felt the day before.

"You look like you've been up all night," I said.

"Yeah."

This time I rolled my eyes.

He caught it. "No, it's not that." He paused and smiled. "Although the sex is amazing."

I held up my hand. "Take pity. I've been flopped on the couch with my kid brother watching porn for two days. I don't need to hear about your earth shattering sex life."

"Sorry. Actually, Scotlyn has been having a lot of nightmares and then she wakes up and she wants to talk about stuff."

"That's good. The poor kid had all of that crap bottled up for years with no one to listen. She'll get better, Nix. She's healing."

I could see the strain of it in his face. "Yeah, I know. And I'm there for her, but sometimes it's painful to hear. She really had it bad, and sometimes, when she doesn't realize I'm looking at her," he smiled to himself, "and believe me, I'm always looking at her, she still looks lost and sad."

"And that's where you come in." Ridiculously, I was better at helping other people understand their feelings. That way it was easier to ignore my own.

Nix nodded. "Yeah, I guess so."

Nix had texted ahead, and Scotlyn was getting her stuff ready to go as we walked in.

Two seconds later, Jason walked out with a hot dog in his hand. His mouth dropped in surprise when he saw me. "I thought you took the day off."

"I did. Just came by to pick up Scotlyn for lunch."

Voices floated out from the back office, and Jason's face twisted. A girl's laugh bounced out next, and the sound of it went straight into my chest. She walked out and froze, the expression on her face mirroring exactly how I felt. Jason had been right. She'd grown up a lot since I'd seen her last. Her incredible copper hair picked up the light coming through the shop window, and I tightened my fist against the urge I had to touch it. The impossibly long pair of tanned legs that had often kept me up at night, stretched out from a pair of jean cut-offs, and I realized I hadn't taken a breath. A guy I'd never seen before walked out next. He was tall and looked like the type that girls went nuts for. Just like Rett, he looked like the kind of guy who was irritatingly comfortable and confident in his skin.

He was oblivious to the thick tension in the room. "You ready to go, Taylor?"

Taylor was still staring at me. Her glossed lips were slightly parted in shock. She ignored him. "Hey." It was the first time I'd ever heard her sound shy. There was nothing shy about Taylor Flinn. Everything about her was like an explosive fireworks show. Just having her stand inside the shop made the place feel different, as if the walls suddenly vibrated with life.

"I just heard you were back in town." I cast a cold glare toward her brother.

She nodded and a trembling smile formed at the edge of her lips. It seemed to occur to her that her boyfriend was standing next to her. "Oh, this is Adam. We were just leaving."

I didn't say another word and crossed my arms, a habit that I'd adopted whenever Taylor was near. As she brushed past me leaving behind the faint scent of her perfume, it dawned on me why I'd always tensed up around her. Nix had teased me about it for a long time, but I'd always ignored him. She was a kid. She was too young, too enticing, and if I'd let Nix's teasing penetrate then I would have had to admit to myself that I wanted her. I'd built a wall, both physically and mentally, and now, it seemed that that wall was coming down brick by brick.

They walked out. Jason avoided looking at me and made the wise decision to finish his hot dog in the backroom. Scotlyn and Nix stared at me, waiting for me to say something, but there was nothing to say.

"Just a minute," I finally growled and headed into the restroom. I leaned down and threw cold water on my face. I braced my hands on the sides of the sink. It sounded as if the whole vanity might come loose. I straightened and took a deep breath before plowing my fist through the bathroom wall. The plaster flaked off in chunks and my knuckles throbbed, but I felt better. I walked out to the front of the shop.

Nix was holding back a smile. "Boy, you were really taking care of business in there."

"Shut the hell up," I said and stormed past him. "Let's go somewhere where they serve beer in pitchers."

CHAPTER 6

Taylor

Adam said something as we climbed into his car, but I had no idea what.

Even after the crappy morning we'd had at the hot dog stand the day before, I'd talked Adam into taking me there again. I'd promised Jason that I would bring him a hot dog, and he'd assured me that Clutch was off for the day. I'd convinced myself that as long as I didn't run into him, I'd be fine. And that might have been true . . . eventually, but seeing him at the shop had started the emotional turmoil and heartbreak all over again. It seemed my whole life had been a series of sadly-ever-after episodes when it came to Clutch. As silly as I was, I'd convinced myself that the guy would come around some day. He knew I was crazy about him, embarrassingly so, and I'd always figured he would feel the same way too if I bugged him enough. And I had definitely bugged him. I had been such a fool. When I thought about my asinine, little girl antics around Clutch and how he'd tensed and scowled whenever I neared him, I realized I'd been completely delusional.

Adam leaned over and kissed me. He could have reached over and slapped me and gotten the same trance-like reaction. "Earth to Taylor."

I forced a smile. "Sorry, I left the planet for a second."

He performed a happy little drumbeat on his steering wheel. "Well, we've got the rest of the afternoon. I don't have to be at work until six. What should we do?" His white teeth gleamed in the sunlight pouring through the windshield. "We could head down to the beach."

"I promised my mom I'd mop floors today." It had been the first lame excuse to come into my head. My stomach felt cold and achy as I pretended that nothing had happened in the shop to throw me into a tailspin, and suddenly, it occurred to me that I'd been way too selfish. Adam had been so cool about everything, always giving in even when it was something he didn't really want to do. As much as I enjoyed being around him, the truth was, I'd been using him badly, both to fill a void and to keep my parents off my back. But just now, in the shop, it had dawned on me that there was no way to fill the Clutch-sized hole in my heart.

Adam started the car. His good mood had been squashed by disappointment. A stiff silence fell between us, and the icky feeling in my stomach grew. Adam fidgeted with the radio and finally shut if off completely.

"That big dude in your brother's shop, that was Clutch, wasn't it?"

I stared out the window at nothing in particular. "Yeah, that's him." The nonchalance in my voice was so contrived, even Adam, who was, in general, not great at reading me, could not have missed it. It was almost as if I could hear the loud cracking sound of the fake shell I'd constructed to keep my parents and Jason off my back. I'd managed, quite skillfully, to fool them into thinking I'd changed, that I'd become the perfectly conforming, well-behaved, good decision maker they'd always dreamed of. And as unhappy as I'd been, I'd tried to persuade myself that it would be all right. Five seconds in the same room with Clutch had destroyed my resolve. Adam deserved way better than me.

"Is it true that you had a thing for the guy?" I'd hoped that my curt answer would have taken him off the subject. He glanced briefly at me. "Some of my friends were talking about it one day."

I didn't answer, which I figured was response enough. He turned up my street and stopped in front of my house, and I really wanted to hop out. But I owed him more than that. "Look, Adam, you know how much I like you—"

"Godammit, Taylor, you aren't actually going to use the *you know how much I like you* line. Save it. I don't want the *you poor guy, I feel so bad for you*, break up. All I know, is everything was fine until you saw your brother's partner. Good luck with that. The guy looks like a total asshole."

"He's not. It's complicated. Adam, I really do have a great time with you, but—"

He stuck up his hand to silence me. "Just stop, Taylor. Go. I don't need your pity."

"Great, I will save my breath then." I opened the door and shot out of his car. His tires screeched as he tore off down the street. Tears burned my eyes as I raced up the driveway. I'd been a terrible bitch about everything, and even though Adam had acted cold and dismissive, I knew I'd just screwed with his head. I'd been forced into becoming someone so far from my true self that I'd momentarily lost the real Taylor. But that was over.

In one of those hard to explain coincidences, I walked in as my mom, clad in yellow rubber gloves, was bent over a bucket squeezing out a mop. Mom had always been one of those mild, conservative, take things slowly decision makers. My parents had dated five years before they'd decided to get married, and something told me it had been a dull, chaste five years. My impulsiveness had always worried her. She'd even considered medication to settle me down, but the doctors had assured her it was just my spirit and nothing more. Even at ten, I'd sensed that it was not the diagnosis she had hoped for.

"You're home already? Why did Adam leave? You should have invited him in. I made some oatmeal cookies." She wiped a strand of her gray flecked hair from her face with the back of her forearm. She hadn't noticed my tear streaked cheeks. I honestly believed that sometimes she ignored any emotional turmoil on my part because it fit better into her quiet, calm life. "Did Jason like his hot dog?"

I shrugged. "I'm sure he did. We didn't stick around to find out. Do you need some help with the floors?" Mom kept an immaculate house. A tidy house was a source of pride for her. Her clean obsession worked well for me because it meant she avoided my 'tornado' room most of the time.

Mom looked down at the gleaming tile beneath her feet. "It's all done now, and besides Dear, you never do it right. You don't switch the water enough, and it always leaves a soapy streak."

"I guess I'll mark cleaning woman off my list of future careers." I trudged toward my room, closed the door behind me and pushed aside the pile of neatly folded clothes Mom had left on my bed. I stared up at the ceiling thinking about everything. I'd left California so heartbroken by Clutch not giving a damn about me being shipped off that I'd decided it was the best thing for me. Being out from under the watchful eye of my parents and Jason and even his nosy-assed girlfriend, Sarah, had been a bonus. But once in Florida, I'd realized there was nothing there for me. I didn't know anyone and Aunt Susan wasn't exactly the type to have a roaring social life, so I'd nearly died of boredom . . . and humidity. When I traveled back for my eighteenth birthday, I decided I would do anything not to have to go back. I'd signed over my soul and my heart just to stay home.

I pushed to my feet and walked over to the one oasis of clean in my room, my desk. I'd organized it with my drawing pencils and sketch pads. Creating fashions with charcoal and colored pencils and then turning them into patterns and garments had kept me from going completely mad whenever I'd gotten grounded. Growing up, it had been a weekly occurrence, and most of the time I'd earned it. But I was an adult now, just six weeks away from graduating high school, and while I still tended to make dumb decisions, I was past the age of being punished.

I opened to a clean sheet of paper and started sketching a short tunic style dress with an extra long belt and short boots. My pencil flew back and forth in short purposeful strokes. The finished product looked like something a medieval girl might wear, maybe even a girl who was waiting for her Viking husband to return from a voyage. Costumes and historical time periods were my favorite. Even though I knew they weren't the type of style that would be flying off the department store shelf, it was what I liked. I ripped the paper off the pad and stuck it on the wall next to the Regency meets goth look I'd created after reading Northanger Abbey in English. The flirty feminine styles of the Jane Austen era were cool but the gothic elements of the novel kept drawing me back to a dark, spicier version of Regency fashion. The whole idea ended up being just a bit too odd and I'd never made it into a pattern. A lot of my stuff was outlandish but someday I planned to design fashion for a living. Naturally, my *supportive*, *open-minded* parents thought my dream of becoming a fashion designer was comical.

I plodded back over to my bed and stretched out. I'd ended things abruptly with Adam, and I would probably be scorned at school for the remainder of my senior year, but I'd done the right thing. In fact, continuing to date him would have been the wrong thing in a lot of ways. Adam was still a big man on campus with or without me, and he would recover quickly. Surely, Facebook was already blowing up with the news, and girls would be pushing each other's posts out of the way to get his attention.

Mom knocked lightly and then poked her head inside. Her cheeks were shiny and red from cleaning floors. "Jason and Sarah are coming for dinner. Why don't you invite Adam?" This thing with Adam had turned my mom into the happiest, sparkliest person in the world.

I opened my mouth to let her know he was working, which was the truth, but it would leave out the unpleasant stuff. Then I decided that, like a stubborn bandage, I just needed to get it over with. "We broke up." I hadn't taken the trouble to sit up or look at her. I just blurted my declaration toward the ceiling.

She pushed the door open and stepped inside, unfortunately. Her hands went on her hips as she stared down at the dress pattern I had pinned over fabric. "This room is a disaster. It's not safe to leave pins on the floor."

I looked over at her. She'd taught me to sew when I was seven. I'd begged her to teach me for a month, and she had finally relented. And it turned out to be some of the best time we'd spent together. "Remember when we sewed that dress for my sixth grade dance, Mom?"

She grunted. "Do I? I've never attempted to work with taffeta again. It was awful."

She'd remembered it as awful, and I'd remembered it as awesome. "We had fun, and it turned out to be the best dress at the dance."

"I guess it wasn't too bad when it was done." She looked over at me and there was a fleeting twinkle of momness in her eyes. "You are so pretty that you could have walked into the dance in a potato sack and still have been the most beautiful girl in the room."

She hadn't said anything like it to me in a long time, and my eyes ached as I kept back tears.

"Anyhow, back to the subject of Adam." She could ruin a moment as quickly as she could build it up. "It was probably just a little spat. He'll get over it soon enough."

"Pollyanna," I muttered under my breath.

"What?"

"Nothing, Mom, but believe me when I tell you it's over. Adam and I are too different."

She nearly tripped on the clothes I'd pushed onto the floor. "I spent a long time folding these things." She bent over to pick them up.

"Leave them, Mom. I'll get them later."

She sat on the edge of my bed. It seemed I was going to be blessed with a heart to heart with her. "Different is a good thing. Opposites attract and all that," she said with a laugh. "Adam will be back, you'll see."

"I broke it off. He's not coming back, and I don't want him to. He's not for me, and I'm definitely not for him."

A long pause filled the air and then an angry sigh broke the silence. "Don't forget the deal, Taylor Marie." Pollyanna had vanished with the revelation that a reunion between Adam and me was not possible. "You need to stay out of trouble."

I leaned up on my elbows. "Really, you're going to resort to the middle name thing. I haven't heard it since I was in eighth grade and I got caught ditching school."

The rosy cheeks and sweet smile were gone and her *mom* scowl darkened her face. Of course, it never had much effect on me, or at least not as much effect as the spine-chilling *dad* scowl. "You know the rules, Kiddo." She stepped over the clothes and headed to the door.

"That's the problem, Mom. I'm not a kid anymore. I'm eighteen. You can kick me out of the house, but you can't tell me where to go, or what to wear, or who to date." I'd made a conscious effort to keep my voice calm, and it threw her for a second. We'd had some pretty good screaming matches during my teen years, but I was not going to let her reduce me to a hysterical teenager. Not anymore.

Her mouth pursed together as she seemed to be formulating her reply. "We'll see what your dad says about that." She spun around sharply on her heels and left the room.

When Mom was done dealing with me she was always more than pleased to hand me off to Dad. It was pretty damn cowardly, but frankly, I was done trying to fit into his mold for the perfect daughter.

CHAPTER 7

Clutch

It was rare for me to lose my appetite, in fact, if there was a word that meant rarer than rare then that would've been the term to use. I'd freaked out both Nix and Scotlyn when I'd hardly touched my burger at lunch. They knew the reason behind it though, and, thankfully, neither of them had brought it up. There wasn't much to talk about. Taylor and I hadn't seen each other in months, and we'd both been caught off guard. I was sure that her stunned reaction had come from fear that she'd broken the 'stay away from Clutch rule' and with Jason standing right there. My reaction had been my usual— construct the wall and try to ignore the fact that every inch of me had reacted to her presence. I guess that hadn't changed. Although, the putting my fist through a wall thing was new.

I turned up my street deciding that I needed a long workout session in the makeshift weight room I'd created in the garage. My hand was sore, but a little pain and sweat seemed just what I needed. I glanced up the street and did a double take when I saw that Barrett was helping my neighbor drag the empty cans back up to her house. He was shirtless, which, knowing my brother, was probably on purpose. Apparently, he'd decided chivalry and a bare chest were a good mix.

Aimee waved at me as I pulled into the driveway. She

was wearing that same glowing smile that I'd seen on so many girls who Barrett had taken the time to talk to. Only hers still came with that sad, lost glaze in her eyes. My brother didn't wave, and I was sure that he would rather not have had me catch him in his act of garbage can valor.

My knuckles and fingers throbbed as I slammed shut the car door. "How's it going, Aimee?"

"Great, James." She was one of the few people who called me James. Aimee was that kind of person, the kind who called people by their proper names. She was polite and well-mannered, and she was stuck with a lazy, classless asshole. "Barrett was kind enough to come out and help me bring in the trash cans."

Barrett finally grew his pair enough to turn around and face me. He waved briefly and then returned his attention to Aimee.

I went inside. Food wrappers and empty beer cans littered my coffee table, and the blankets were on the floor where Barrett had apparently thrown them, deciding that the bedroom was too far to travel to on foot. The front door opened and Barrett stepped inside without making eye contact.

I crossed my arms and watched him slink toward the couch. "I guess you think if you don't look directly at me then I won't be able to see you."

"No, but I can already sense a lecture in the air," he waved his arm around. "You reek of it."

"And you reek of the neighbor's trash can," I lifted my nose and sniffed, "and some of my expensive aftershave. So, you had time to put on aftershave but not a shirt?"

He shrugged and it was that kind of kid brother shrug that was not going to sit well with my mood. "A guy likes to smell good when he's taking in the garbage cans." He plopped on the couch and propped his feet between an empty beer can and an open bag of chips.

I picked up two of the cans and crushed them in my hands, forgetting about my swollen fingers.

Barrett's blue eyes went wide as if he'd envisioned his head in my fist instead of the can. "Bad day?"

"As a matter of fact, yes. And what the hell are you doing? Or did you not hear me mention that she was married?"

"Yeah, to a humongous asshole." He pointed at me, and I noticed that most of the tremble was gone. "Your words, not mine. Besides, I like to be helpful."

My rumbling laugh startled him, assuring me that he was still slightly on edge. "Since when are you helpful?"

He lifted his arms and rested his hands behind his head. "Always— as long as a cute girl is involved."

"Then be helpful and clean this mess up. I'm going out to lift weights."

"You're definitely not cute enough," Barrett called to me as I walked out the back door.

***

A grueling session of weights was always a stress reliever, but it hadn't dulled my senses when it came to Taylor. A few seconds in the same room with her and it was as if I'd held her in my arms and tasted her lips. I couldn't seem to pile on enough weights or do enough reps to push her from my head.

A rhythmic pounding on the kitchen wall greeted me as I grabbed a paper towel to wipe my face. It continued. I stepped into the living room. Barrett was sitting on the coffee table amongst his collection of litter throwing an old tennis ball against the wall. It had left a nice mark where he'd managed to hit the same exact spot numerous times. He'd been a talented pitcher in high school, but he'd never had enough self-discipline to continue in the sport.

"You're leaving a fucking mark on the wall." He'd only been here a week, but I'd been living on my own for two years and his presence was getting on my nerves fast.

He ignored me and threw the ball again but I snatched it from mid air.

He leaned back on his hands and an empty chip bag floated to the floor, leaving a nice shower of salt on the rug. "What the hell am I going to do now, Jimmy? I have no diploma or job. I was making good money on the fishing boat. It was hard work but it paid well. Don't know what to do now."

"You could go to night school and get your diploma."

He snorted a laugh. "I'm not going to sit in any fucking classroom ever again."

I tossed the ball up and down on my palm. "You could dress real sexy and stand on the street corner. Maybe some rich woman will pick you up like in that Pretty Woman movie."

He wasn't amused. "I'm serious. I'm screwed."

"You screwed yourself, Rett."

He got up to retrieve the trash he'd dumped on the floor.

"Maybe I should get back into baseball. The coach always thought I had big potential."

I collected up the empty cans. "I believe his exact words were 'too bad about Barrett, he had big potential.' You screwed up that opportunity too."

He swept up the blankets and threw them on the couch. "This little chat is a big boost to my confidence." He looked at me. "Maybe I should just get back into drugs. Then I can sell—"

His last word was sucked away by a gasp as I took three steps across the room and pinned him against the wall. My forearm pressed against his chest, and he looked as scared as I'd ever seen him. The strain of the day— hell, of the whole goddamn week had gotten to me.

"I love you, Rett, but if you ever get hooked again, I will throw you into the fucking street."

He blinked at me a few times. "I wouldn't do that to you, Jimmy. I wouldn't let you down like that. I was only kidding."

I stared down at him and then I dropped my arm. It had been an overreaction, but at the same time, scaring the shit out of him was probably a good thing. I nodded. "Let me talk to Jason about hiring you to work part time at the shop. We could use an extra pair of hands."

"That'd be great." There was still a slight tremble in his voice. He began cleaning the rest of the room, a bonus side effect of my small tantrum.

I walked over to grab my cell phone from the table.

Barrett glanced down at it as I reached for it. "What happened to your hand?"

"It had an argument with a wall."

"We all make bad choices. By the way, someone's been trying to call you. Your phone has been doing the cha-cha across the table for a half hour."

I glanced at the screen. "It was Jason." I was glad he'd left a message. I really didn't want to talk to the guy.

"Hey, Clutch, we've got a lead on a sixty-five Shelby GT350. It's a wreck and has to be remodeled from the chassis up, but it could be a great investment. The guy is going to the classic car meet-up tonight. I can't make it, but you're better at striking deals anyhow. Call me and I'll give you all the info."

"Why did you argue with a wall?" Barrett asked as I lowered the phone. "I'm figuring after the weights I heard being shifted around in the garage and having you pancake me against the wall that something has you really tense."

"None of your business, Rett, and this place better sparkle. I want to see my reflection in that coffee table." Seconds before, he'd looked terrified enough to swallow his own tongue, but my brother had the unbelievable confidence that allowed him to recuperate quickly. Growing up with four older brothers had given him amazing survival skills. He flipped on the stereo and then folded the comforters.

"Those need to go into the washer," I said. "You've been sweating, barfing and doing other things I don't want to think about in those blankets for a week."

He nodded and gathered them up under his arm. "I'm thinking it's all about a girl."

I waved him toward the laundry room. "Stop trying to

psychoanalyze me. Don't turn on the washer yet. I'm taking a shower. I've got to see a guy about a car." I walked into the hallway.

"And I'll bet the girl's initials are T. F.," he called to me. I had to admit, the kid had a steel pair of balls. "Because everyone knows that Taylor was meant for you. Everyone but you, that is."

I shut the bathroom door behind me.

CHAPTER 8

Taylor

I woke to the sound of voices. I'd fallen asleep long enough for the bright sunlight of the day to fade to the faint pink light of dusk. The dim glow of the dying sun seeped beneath my bedroom blinds. The day came back to me in slivers, but one fragment was lodged painfully in my mind and my heart— I'd stood in the same room with Clutch, and I was still crazy about him.

There had been so many times in the past few years that I'd tried to figure out why I was so nuts about him considering that he'd always treated me like shit. I'd been convinced that if I thought about it logically then I could just as easily talk myself out of the crush. But this had never been a crush, this had never been a school girl's obsession with a monstrously built, good-looking guy who drove fast cars. James Mason had a soul that sometimes I was sure only I could see. He was a guy who would do anything for his friends and family even if it meant putting himself in danger, and somewhere deep in my bones, I was sure that he would risk everything for me too. Even though he'd always been irritated at my very presence, I'd kept that hope inside of me. Something deep within drove me to the guy as if there was only one person in the world for me, and if Clutch didn't want me I was sure I'd spend the rest of my life alone.

Mom's harsh knock startled me out of my thoughts. "Dinner is ready, Taylor. Jason and Sarah are here." She stuck her head inside. She'd put on a dress and pearls as if Jason and Sarah were important dinner guests. Her lips pulled tight, and it was obvious there was something she needed to confess. "I called Adam."

I sat straight up. "You what?"

She put up her hand. "He's not coming. He had to work."

I took a deep breath to keep my cool, but she was making it extremely hard. "Mom," the icy tone in my voice caught her attention quickly, "he's never coming here again. We are through and don't ever fucking call him again."

I'd spoken quietly, but, almost as if he had some kind of bad language radar, my dad popped his head in over hers. "What did I just hear you say to your mother?"

Mom turned around and placed her hand against his chest. "It was nothing, Carl. Just girl talk." She'd extinguished the potential explosion quickly, not out of worry about me but out of worry that her little dinner party would be disrupted.

Dad hesitated in the doorway and shot me an admonishing glare before walking away. Mom's face was a shade paler as she stared hard at me from across the room. "Get changed out of those trashy shorts and come to the table. We'll talk about this later."

I could hear Jason discussing a classic car meet and an investment opportunity as I trudged down the hallway.

"Do you think Jimmy will be able to—" Dad snapped his mouth shut as I entered the dining room. Apparently, I was not even allowed to hear a conversation about Clutch.

I scraped the feet of the chair along Mom's sparkling floor as I yanked it from the table and sat down hard.

"Don't slouch, Taylor," Mom said sounding like Mrs. Biddle, my witch-faced second grade teacher. I over exaggerated a ramrod straight posture and plopped my elbows on the table. These people still treated me like a bratty, little girl, so I decided to roll with it. Mom's eyes nearly bulged out of her head when she saw me place my elbows on the table.

Jason smacked my arm, and I dropped back into the slouch. "So, Mom said you had a little fight with Adam?"

I smiled and shook my head. "Wasn't a little fight. We're through. Not that I see any reason why I have to discuss this with you."

Sarah's mouth dropped but Jason quickly placed a hand on her arm to stop her from commenting.

Mom picked up the potato bowl and handed it to me. "Let's pass the potatoes around. I added some parmesan cheese to them, so they should be extra tasty." Pollyanna had returned but I knew better. I knew that the anti-polly could emerge at a moment's notice. She was almost scarier than Dad because with him he was always pissed off about something. He never put on the fake shit, and at the moment, his jaw twitched with anger.

"When did you break up with Adam?" He looked questioningly at Mom. "And why did no one tell me?"

Mom shrugged as she spooned peas and carrots onto her plate. "I was going to tell you after dinner. Besides, I'm sure it will all work itself out."

I laughed loudly, another no-no at the dinner table. I

knew that everything I was doing would get me into deep trouble, but I could no longer play along with their creepy little game. "I had no idea that my dating life was such an important topic. Really you people need to get lives. And, nothing is going to work itself out, Mom. I was using Adam and it was wrong, so I broke it off."

Mom turned to me looking like a woman who'd been inhaling far too many cleaning chemicals. "What do you mean you were using him? For what?"

"To keep all of you off my back." I smiled to myself. "Although, Adam didn't keep me off my ba—"

Jason stood so abruptly his chair nearly flew back. "Taylor, we need to talk out in the kitchen." I was waiting for fire to come squirting from his nostrils. "Now."

I walked casually behind him to the kitchen, but I could have bounced a dime off the tension in his shoulders. He shut the kitchen door behind us and flew around to face me. Still no flames but I was sure I saw a stream of smoke drifting out of his ears.

"What the hell are you doing? You're going to get shipped back to Florida. Is that what you want?"

I stared at him and he seemed flustered by my silence.

"This is all about running into Clutch today, isn't it?" He shook his head. "I shouldn't have asked for that hot dog."

I laughed and it made him even angrier. "Really, you're blaming a hot dog for my behavior? That's about as stupid as blaming Clutch for it. You people are truly nuts, do you know that? You and Mom and Dad and that sniveling little witch you live with—"

He grabbed my wrist hard, and I met his glare with one

of my own. "I hope they do send you back. You're nothing but trouble. And give up on Jimmy. He's told me a million times that you were nothing but a pain in the ass. He has no interest in a stupid kid like you." He dropped my wrist and headed to the door. "Now come back to the table." He slammed out of the kitchen.

I stood in the middle of Mom's immaculate kitchen and blinked back tears. His last words had hurt way more than I'd prepared myself for. There was no way I was sitting back down at that table. I stormed out the back door and ran down to the sidewalk and down the street away from the crazy house and the people inside who spent all of their waking hours making me miserable.

CHAPTER 9

Clutch

Nix was looking over a late 1980's Mercedes as I crossed the lot with Barrett in tow. He'd felt well enough to go and like a wild, untrained puppy, I was worried that he'd destroy the house if I left him alone too long.

Nix pushed his sunglasses onto his head. "Hey, Barrett, you look a lot better."

"Rett!" Dray called from across the way. He jogged over and gave Barrett a quick bro hug. "Good to see you, Bud."

"Yeah, you too. Won any good fights lately?" Barrett asked.

"You know it. Victory is always mine in the ring."

Nix looked over at Dray. "Unless you leave brain matter on the mat and end up in the hospital."

Dray waved Nix off. "Anyhow, you'll have to come watch a match I'm in later this month. Should be a good one."

"Definitely."

Dray smacked Nix on the arm with the back of his hand. "Hey, Pal, can you spot me a twenty. Cassie has me on a budget so we can eventually buy a place, and I've decided to eat my way through the entire line of food trucks. The macaroni and cheese truck is my next target. I'm going for the lobster mac and cheese, and it's expensive."

Nix went to pull out his wallet and then stopped. "Why don't you just get the plain mac and cheese?"

Dray held up his hands. "Because it's lobster, Dude. Now, come on. Don't be such a friggin' tightwad."

"I'm glad this budget is working out for you," Nix muttered as he dragged out his wallet and handed Dray money.

Nix shook his head as Dray dashed off.

"Hey, you've got your burden. . . " I inclined my head toward Barrett. ". . . and I've got mine."

"Thanks a lot," Barrett growled. "I'm going to catch up with Dray and leave you two old ladies to yourselves."

Nix looked at me. "Shit, is he right? Cause I'm starting to feel a little old ladyish."

"Nah, they just haven't grown up yet. Hey, I'm glad you came. There's some guy out here named Grant who has a sixty-five Shelby for sale. He's supposed to be showing a seventy-nine Ferrari tonight."

"Yeah, I saw him over near the restrooms." Nix started walking and I followed.

"Where's Scotlyn?"

"I left her sitting on deck, huddled in a blanket with her computer and cat on her lap. Since she's been helping Nana write her memoirs, she's decided to write her own. I read some stuff she wrote. It's pretty damn good. Tears my heart out to read it but she's a good writer. Her doctor told her it was great therapy."

"That's awesome. Hey, so that stray cat stuck around?"

"Yeah. He's a cool cat, but he did deliver a dead rat into

our bed the other morning." Nix laughed. "Boy, can Scotlyn scream when she puts her mind to it."

"Shit, if I woke up staring at a dead rat I'd scream too." I spotted the yellow Ferrari. "Nothing like restoring a fucking Ferrari and then painting it the color of piss," I said out of the corner of my mouth as we approached the guy. He was an old dude with a gray ponytail and a straw fedora, and I briefly wondered if that was the way I would look in thirty years.

I stuck out my hand. "Are you Grant?"

We shook hands. "Yep, and my friend, Felix, did not exaggerate in his description. He told me to look for a man the size of a grizzly bear with blond hair."

I'd been a giant all my life and I'd grown used to having people mention my size, but, I had to admit, the grizzly bear analogy always felt like an insult. But I was here to relieve this guy of his Shelby so I grinned in response to his comment.

"I'm Jimmy, but most people call me Clutch. I understand you have a sixty-five Shelby you need to sell."

The guy walked over and blew an invisible speck of dust off his Ferrari. "Well, I don't *need* to sell it, but if I got the right price I might be willing to part with it."

From what Jason had told me, the guy was having some financial troubles, and he definitely needed to unload stock. But he was a pro and the number one rule was never let your customer know you're desperate.

"Do you have any pictures?"

"It just so happens that I do." He ducked inside his car.

I glanced around the lot but there was no sign of Barrett.

I looked at Nix. "Do you think the kids are all right on their own?"

Nix laughed and shook his head. "I doubt it. For Dray, having your brother back in town is like a stick of dynamite finding his long lost fuse."

Grant returned with the photos. He shuffled through them, obviously looking for the most flattering. "Here she is. My pride and joy."

Fortunately, I was a pro too, and I knew how to look disgusted and disappointed on the outside even if my insides were doing a 'got to have this car' dance. The car looked as if it had been sitting in a swamp for ten years followed by another decade in the desert sun. And she was fucking awesome. "I'll give you forty thousand."

The guy laughed. "Don't insult me."

"Look, I'm going to need a hundred grand just to get her moving again." Which was completely true, but, man, would it be worth that hundred grand.

The guy twisted his mouth and looked back at the pictures as if he'd forgotten what the car looked like. "Nope, can't do it."

If I'd had to choose to leave without the Shelby deal or my left arm, I'd be sawing through bone at this moment. I kept my *I can't even believe I'm bothering to make an offer* face. "Forty-five or I'm walking."

The guy sighed as if he was no longer interested in talking to me, and I was quickly calculating just how high I could go before losing my ass completely. Then he stared up at me from beneath the brim of his hat. "Let me call my partner and see." I'd been around long enough to know that when an old guy said he had to check with his partner, it meant he had to clear it with the wife.

"All right, call your *partner*. My friend and I will be right over there."

Nix followed me over to a tree that was out of earshot of the guy. "I've got to have that car," I said quietly.

"Yeah, I gathered that."

I looked over at him. "How could you tell? I was putting on my best poker face." Now I worried that my desperation had leaked through my stiff expression.

"It's not how you look. It's how you sound." He smiled and placed a hand on my shoulder. "Dude, when you're dealing and you want something badly, your voice goes up a couple of octaves."

"What are you saying, that I sound like a girl when I'm making a deal?"

"Only when it's something you really want. And it would take more than a few octaves for you to sound like a girl, but you do kind of remind me of Mrs. Hatter, the geometry teacher, who used to get all excited when she was teaching something complicated, which, in geometry, was every day." He smiled. "It's all right to get in touch with your feminine side every once in awhile. Even if you're a *grizzly*."

The guy was still on the phone, which could have been good or bad. "Feminine side, bullshit. Besides, you're the one everyone calls pretty."

Nix rubbed the back of his neck. "Yeah, I don't know which is worse, grizzly or pretty. But now that Barrett is back, maybe I can hand the pretty title over. He sort of stepped into my shoes once you and I left high school."

"Nothing pisses him off more than to be called pretty." The old guy was off the phone and glancing around for us. He must have been nearsighted because I was hard to miss.

"Well, it looks like we have a deal at forty-five."

I kept up my stiff, non-committal exterior and held back the Tarzan yell that was lodged in my throat. We shook on it and made arrangements to meet at the bank in the morning. I'd needed this to go well. Rotten shit had been happening all week, and this had definitely brought me out of my funk.

Nix peered sideways at me as we walked away and laughed. "It's all right if you want to do a victory dance. I don't think the guy could see too well."

I punched the air. "I'm so fucking jazzed right now, I don't even mind talking to Jason." I pulled out my phone. "And since the money is half his. . . "

Nix stopped. "I'm going over to the pastrami truck. Do you want me to order you a sandwich?"

"Yeah, but get me two." I dialed Jason. "I'll be over there in a second." The great weather had brought a big crowd, and between the music blaring from car radios and the conversations drifting around me, I couldn't hear a thing. I walked through the maze of people to the gray brick building that housed the bathrooms. Jason didn't answer so I left a message. "Hey, I got it at forty-five—"

She came around the corner, unexpectedly and like a hurricane of stars. My mind went completely blank. I hung up and stuck the phone in my pocket.

Taylor's long lashes curtained her smooth cheeks as she dropped her gaze.

The adrenaline rush left behind from getting my hands on a Shelby morphed into an explosion of every emotion I'd ever felt. I lunged forward and grabbed her hand. She gasped as I dragged her around the back of the building. I pressed her up against the bricks and stared down at her.

Her chin jutted forward as she lifted her face to me and then without warning her hand came up and she slapped me hard. I didn't move but my face stung plenty.

"You could have cared less when my parents shipped me off." Her eyes glistened with tears.

I shook my head. "Not true, Taylor. It was just easier—"

She slapped me again. "It was easier for me to be gone." She was not a girl that cried easily, but now the tears streamed down her cheeks.

This time I stretched open my mouth to get the sting out. "Shit, Taylor, would you let me talk." I grabbed hold of her arms. "It was easier for me not to say good-bye." And then every suppressed urge I'd ever had to kiss her, and there had been many, erupted. My fingers squeezed her thin arms as I lifted her toward me. My mouth devoured hers and any ounce of self-control was gone. I pulled her so hard against me, she groaned softly against my mouth. As my mind warned me against it, my hands smoothed over the slim curve of her hips and bottom, the sweet little bottom that I'd dreamt about countless times. She leaned harder against me, assuring me that I could have her completely. And there was nothing I wanted more. But it was far more complicated than that. Breathless, I reluctantly pulled my mouth from hers and wrapped my arms around her.

"Do you know how long I've waited for you to do that," she said softly against my neck.

"I doubt as long as I've wanted to do it." I rested my chin on the top of her head, but she pulled away to stare up at me.

Her perfect, plump lips looked swollen from the kiss. "Why didn't you ever kiss me then?"

"You're Jason's kid sister, Taylor. You were young. The whole thing was kind of warped."

She lifted her arm but I grabbed her wrist before her hand made contact with my face. "You're a damn coward," she said. "I would have risked anything, even being thrown out of the house, if it meant being with you."

I combed my hair back out of my face and my shoulders relaxed with a sigh. "I wasn't a coward, Taylor." I should have opted for the slap. It would have been far less painful than having her call me a coward. I tried to choose my words carefully, but it never seemed to matter. With Taylor, I always managed to find the exact wrong thing to say. "It was about doing what was right." And her expression assured me that I'd nailed it again.

"So being with me would have been wrong?"

I stepped back. "Shit, you're twisting my words. Maybe you're just too young to understand." My first words were wrong, but my last ones were the death knell.

"Go to hell, Clutch." She stormed away in the pissed off style that she'd perfected.

I momentarily stared at the brick wall in front of me but then decided it would hurt a lot more than plaster. What the hell was with my luck lately?

My phone rang as I rounded the building and plowed back into the melee of people and shiny chrome. I ignored it. Taylor had managed to disappear completely.

Nix spotted me and headed over with the food. He stopped in front of me and lifted a brow as he noticed my face. "I heard handprint was the new thing in skin art." He leaned his head to get a better look. "And from the looks of it, I'd say you took a double hit. What did you do in your excitement? Grab the first girl you saw?" I didn't answer and his cocky smile disappeared. He glanced around and then looked back up at me. "She's here?"

"Yep, and I don't want to talk about it."

He held up the sandwich. "Still interested in the pastrami?"

I grabbed it from him. "Yes. At the moment, food is my only source of joy." I ripped open the paper and spotted Dray wandering through the crowd alone as I shoved the sandwich in my mouth. Even in a thick crowd of people, my head stuck out like a beacon on a lighthouse. He saw me and headed over.

"Where the hell is Barrett?" I was not in the mood to deal with any of my brother's antics. "If he has climbed into the backseat of some girl's car then he's going to have to find his own way home tonight."

"Nah, he was behind me, but he stopped to answer his phone." Dray stared longingly at my sandwich. "I didn't see the pastrami truck. Where was it hiding?"

Nix pointed behind his shoulder. "Right back there in the middle of the lot with the big plastic pastrami sandwich on top. You're really thinking of following up lobster with pastrami?"

Dray scrunched his face and pressed his hand against his

stomach. "Yeah, maybe it's too much." Then he glanced up at me and leaned his head to one side just like Nix had done. "It looks like you ran into a hand."

"Sort of." I stared down at my half eaten sandwich and realized that even food wasn't bringing any relief from my misery. This thing with Taylor made no sense and was completely out of whack and I had no idea how to fix it. All I knew was that all this time I'd been denying myself the one thing I wanted more than anything, more than any car, more than any racing win, more than any damn pastrami sandwich. I wanted Taylor Flinn, and I was never going to be completely happy without her. I shoved the sandwich into Dray's hand. "Here you go. Enjoy. I'm going to round up my *kid* and head home."

CHAPTER 10

Taylor

I'd bummed a ride off of friends to get to the car meet, but I had no way to get home. I'd run out of the house without my phone. Cell phones were forbidden at the dinner table, so I'd left it behind on my nightstand. Not that I wanted to go back home. I was going to be in for a major scene with both parents, and I had no doubt that they'd try to send me back to Florida.

Fortunately, I'd defied my mom's orders to change out of my *trashy* shorts. Jason had given me a twenty for the hot dog and told me to keep it for my troubles. This seemed like definite trouble. I had no place to go at the moment, and with the fragile state my last encounter with Clutch had left me in, the last thing I needed was a parent lecture.

I headed down the street to the bus stop. I didn't even care where the bus was headed. I just needed to get on and ride. The entire scene came back to me. It seemed like I'd been waiting my entire life for that kiss, and every second of it had been as mind-blowing as I'd imagined. But it had ended in the same way all my incidences with Clutch had ended, with a dull, heavy ache in my chest. Only now it felt as if all the hurt I'd endured these past two years had swelled up into one giant heartbreak. The word *coward* had shot out before I could stop myself. But to hear that after all this time he'd wanted to kiss me but hadn't, in fact, he'd gone out of his way to prove to me that he wanted nothing to do with me, it had been too much. I'd lashed out at him, but, truthfully, I wasn't sorry I'd done it. Maybe Clutch needed to see what it felt like to ache for someone so badly you were nearly sick from it. That was how it had been for me these past two years. If he'd wanted me, he should have been true to himself, instead of trying to 'do the right thing'. I knew him well enough to know that he'd never been an angel. He'd gotten into plenty of trouble growing up, but when it came to me, he was like a damn saint.

I reached the bus stop bench just as a bus came around the corner. The sign above the windshield said Ocean Boulevard.

I climbed on board and headed to the back of the bus. At night, city buses were filled with weary looking people who were just anxious to get home after a long day's work. Tonight was no different. I found an empty seat and climbed in behind a woman who smelled as if she'd been working in a strawberry jam factory all day. It smelled good to me, but I could only imagine how the lady felt about strawberry jam after wearing it all day. The smell of fruit and my lack of dinner made my stomach growl, and I pressed my arm into my gut to quiet it.

What a day of crap it had been. My head felt like lead from it all. The rhythmic motion of the bus, as it careened from side to side along the rough stretches of pothole dotted streets, lulled me into deep thought. Maybe I was screwing myself. Everything had been going along quietly and without emotional upheaval until today. I could have just stayed in my pretend state of being normal and ignored all of my feelings and passion and happiness. I could have remained in the dull frozen world of pleasing my family.

A cool breeze drifted through the slightly lowered bus windows. We were nearing the coast. I scooted down and hugged myself for warmth and closed my eyes. I thought about the brief heated moments I'd spent wrapped in Clutch's arms. Twice before I'd been in those incredibly massive arms, and both times I'd felt instantly comforted as if nothing could ever harm me as long as his arms were around me.

When I'd run away from home and spent a long night out on the streets, the only person I'd wanted to see was Clutch. I'd been a silly, stupid kid thinking I was tough enough to brave it out on my own, and it had scared me shitless. I was in such a sorry state and I'd felt so foolish and sad that the moment I saw Clutch I dropped into his embrace. I'd wanted to stay there forever, but, eventually, he let go. As much as I'd wanted him, he'd been just as eager to hand me back to my family. And when I'd followed another ridiculous impulse and had driven off in and destroyed Clutch's car, I was sure he would be furious at me. Instead, he'd pulled me into his arms. At the time I'd convinced myself that his reaction proved that he loved me, but I was too good at growing fantasies in my head. Now I was done with it. I was done chasing Clutch. If he wanted me he'd have to do the chasing, and I was pretty sure hell would freeze up like an ice pop before that ever happened.

My weary mind had formulated a plan to sleep on the beach, even if it might have been a little cold down on the sand, but then another thought popped into my head. I was feeling beyond distraught, and I knew there was only one person who I could talk to who would listen without judgment and without handing out unwanted advice. I needed to talk to Scotlyn.

I walked along the boardwalk to the harbor. A salty fog brushed lightly over the beach, and I shivered in the cold mist. Aside from two people walking arm and arm and a few stray bicyclists on the walkway, the beach was deserted. I was glad to reach the dock where Nix's boat was anchored.

The soft clanging of metal and the slapping of water against the hulls was the only other sound. I could see someone sitting on deck as I neared the Zany Lucy, and I was relieved to see Scotlyn's blonde hair glowing in the moonlight. She spun around as she heard my footsteps on the wooden planks of the pier. I lifted my hand to wave.

It took her a second to recognize me through the haze. "Taylor," she said with surprise and then she leaned to the side to see if anyone one was with me.

"I'm all alone." My tone sounded foreign and weak to my ears, and the vast ocean landscape seemed to swallow it up completely.

"Come on board, Sweetie. I was just heading in for some cocoa. The fog has finally seeped beneath the blanket. Even the cat went inside."

I stepped onto the deck. The movement of the boat made me feel clumsy and insecure. Scotlyn seemed to sense my unease. She tucked her laptop under one arm and held out her other hand for me to take. Her fingers were cold. We stepped into the tiny cabin.

I'd been on the Zany Lucy several times before, and it'd always taken me a few minutes to get over the claustrophobic feeling it gave me. My long legs could take me across the living room in eight steps, and though I'd never been on the boat at the same time as Clutch, I could only imagine how ridiculous he would look inside it.

Scotlyn dropped her blanket on the back of the couch and placed her laptop on the table. I followed her into the tiny mouse hole they called a kitchen.

"How is the writing coming?" I asked.

She reached into a cupboard and pulled out a box of cocoa. "Some days are better than others." She turned around and I always marveled at how amazingly pretty she was, even without any make-up. "Sometimes I sit down and my fingers can't keep up with everything I want to write, and other days, I stare at the monitor hoping some magical little word fairy will pop up and tell me what to type."

I smiled at the image. "If only there really were fairies. Cinderella didn't know how good she had it."

Scotlyn laughed as she poured the cocoa powder into cups. She glanced down as her cat circled her legs. "There you are. You always seem to come out of hiding when I'm in this kitchen." She stuck a pot of water on the stove and motioned for me to have a chair at the table. "You seem like the marshmallow type."

I nodded. "Absolutely. And a double layer please. It's been a rough night."

She plucked the bag of marshmallows and tossed them on the table. "I usually keep adding them until I'm down to the last drop of cocoa."

I opened the bag, took out two marshmallows, and pushed them into my mouth. "Who needs the cocoa?"

Scotlyn pulled up a chair across from me. "What's happened, Taylor? You don't seem like yourself."

My throat tightened and I took a deep breath because the last thing I wanted to do was break down into a sorry-ass sob session. "Well, my parents are medieval, my brother is far too interested in my life and Clutch—" I shoved another marshmallow into my mouth, but the words still popped out. "Clutch kissed me."

Scotlyn smiled. "About time. That guy was going to explode soon otherwise."

Her reaction surprised me. "But he hates me. He's always made it clear that I am a complete and utter nuisance."

Steam rose from the pot on the stove, and she swiveled around in her chair and grabbed it. She poured hot water into the cups, and we covered our cocoas with a layer of marshmallows.

"Trust me, Clutch does not hate you." She sipped her cocoa. "That hits the spot. I was concentrating so hard out there, I hadn't noticed that a cold fog had floated in until my fingers were too numb to type."

I slurped off the warm foam. "But he does consider me a nuisance. In fact, he's told me that many times."

"Maybe. But he has a whole different reason for it than you think."

"Well, I'm done with him. I'm done making a fool of myself when it comes to James Mason. I don't need him."

"That's the spirit." Scotlyn lifted her mug, and we clinked them together in a toast.

Some of the hot drink spilled onto my thumb, and I licked it off.

"Besides," Scotlyn said, "sometimes a little cold shoulder is the best way to get their attention."

"I gave him way more than a cold shoulder tonight. I slapped him really hard. Twice."

Scotlyn pressed the back of her hand against her mouth to avoid spitting out the mouthful of cocoa. She swallowed. "Really?"

I lifted my hand. "Hurt like hell. It was like smacking my hand against a brick wall."

She burst out laughing just as Nix walked in. His amber eyes rounded as he stepped in and saw me sitting at the table. "Taylor?" He glanced around as if someone could be hiding in his shoebox sized living room. "Who did you come with?"

"No one."

"She came to see me," Scotlyn spoke up, "and we're having a girl chat." She flicked her hand. "So, off you go."

"Fine, fine, but that looks good." He leaned over the table, took long sip of her cocoa, and headed to the bedroom.

"Do you mind if I crash on your couch tonight?" I asked. "I don't have money to get home, and something tells me my return is not going to be met with a welcome home party. I left on pretty ugly terms. Jason and Sarah were over for dinner—"

Scotlyn lifted her hand. "Say no more. I've met Sarah. Of course you can stay, but you've got to tell your parents you're here. Even medieval parents worry." Scotlyn's smile was one of those that made you feel like everything was going to be all right even if you'd just had a terrible night and the guy you loved more than anything in the world had left with *your* handprint on his face and *his* handprint on your heart.

CHAPTER 11

Clutch

"It's only nine o'clock," Barrett said. "We should hit a couple of clubs. I've been sleeping so much, I'm wide awake." He'd been amped up since we'd left the car meet, and it seemed to have had something to do with the phone call. He never mentioned who he'd been talking to and I hadn't asked, mostly because I couldn't have cared less. I had my own shit to deal with, and I had no time for, or interest in, Barrett's crap.

"I've got to work tomorrow. I'm not going anywhere."

"Figures," he sighed. "Some things never change."

"What the hell is that supposed to mean?"

He shrank down in the seat and reached for the radio, but I blocked his hand. "You're right, Rett. Nothing ever changes. You are still the same selfish brat you've always been. Must be fucking nice to live in your carefree world with no worries or concerns. Oh, except, when you are strung out and you have no place else to go and then I've got to step in and save your sorry ass."

"Yes, the almighty, powerful Clutch has once again saved the world. Get over yourself, Jimmy."

My fingers turned white as they tightened around the steering wheel. One good tug and I could have snapped it off. I shook my head. "I don't need this from you tonight,

Rett. So just shut the hell up."

He sat silently and stared out the window the rest of the trip home. I yanked into the driveway and threw the car into park. In my fury, I hadn't noticed the flickering front lights next door, and I hadn't heard the sound of the lawnmower or smelled freshly cut grass until I climbed out of the car. Barrett was halfway to Aimee's front lawn before I could say a word.

My petite neighbor was trudging across the front yard behind the lawn mower at nine o'clock at night while her imbecile husband stood on the porch smoking a cigarette. I could see the tension in Barrett's shoulders as he stormed over to the small wall that separated our two driveways. Aimee hadn't seen him standing there, but Dustin lowered his cigarette and glared at Barrett from across the yard.

I caught up with Barrett just as Dustin opened his mouth to speak. "What are you looking at pretty boy?"

Barrett glanced at me. "Did that sonavabitch just call me pretty boy?"

"Look, Rett, this is only going to make things worse for her." I reached for his arm, but he yanked it away.

"Are you kidding me?" Barrett yelled across the lawn. "What kind of an asshole lets his wife mow the lawn?"

Aimee had turned the mower around and now saw the scene unfolding behind her. Her face stiffened as she looked from Barrett to Dustin and back again.

Dustin walked to the edge of the porch, but being the weasel that he was, he stayed close to the house. He took a long draw on his cigarette, dropped it to the ground, and extinguished it with his shoe. "Why don't you come over here and say that, Blondie?" The second the threat left his mouth, he seemed to regret it. Even beneath his unstable porch light, I could see the pallor of his skin lighten.

Barrett hopped the dividing wall and strode with long, hard steps across the lawn with his fists clenched. Dustin backed up but didn't scurry inside like I was sure he would. Aimee turned off the mower and stared wide-mouthed at Barrett. My even longer strides took me over the wall and to the porch before Rett was able to throw a punch. I grabbed his arm. His muscle pulsed with anger beneath my grasp. With my brother restrained, Dustin worked up enough courage to step forward.

White hot rage circled the three of us as we glared at each other in an almost comical front porch stand-off.

Then a sweet, shaky voice jarred all of us. "What's going on here?"

Barrett relaxed but only slightly. I was certain he would not throw a fist at Dustin with Aimee standing so close. The cold look my brother shot me as I released him assured me that he was now more pissed at me than at the asshole cowering on the porch.

Dustin also seemed to sense that he was safe with Aimee standing right behind us. "Well, Mason, are you going to get this fucker off my property, or should I call the police?"

I snorted. "*Your* property? You wish." I glanced back at the lawn mower. "The fact that you aren't feeling the slightest bit embarrassed about this astounds me. You are an even bigger asshole than I thought. And believe me, I thought you were a humongous one."

Dustin's nostrils flared. I knew none of this was helping Aimee.

Barrett spun around to leave and stopped in front of Aimee. She looked up at him with round blue eyes, and there was a hint of admiration and thankfulness in them. "You deserve way better than this, Aimee."

"Just get off my property, you jerk, and let me worry about how I take care of my wife," Dustin sneered, obviously believing that I was there as an added wall of protection.

Instead, the stress of the night had gotten to me. I jumped over three steps and in less than a second I was toe to toe with him, standing close enough to smell his rancid cigarette breath as he turned his face up to me. The few shades of color left behind from his encounter with Barrett had gone completely.

I kept my fists to my side, but my tone made up for it. "When we leave here, you do not take this out on her, do you understand? Because if you do, if you lay one hand on her or even raise your voice to her, I will be back over here so fast, you won't have time piss your pants."

Dustin licked his thin lips nervously and his gaze flitted to Aimee.

"You guys should just go." There was a tremor in Aimee's voice.

I felt sick about the whole thing. Barrett had been trying to do the right thing, but, as usual, he'd acted before thinking. I was just as pissed at Barrett as I was at the douchebag standing in front of me.

I leaned in closer so that only Dustin could hear. "Understand me?"

"Just get off my porch," Dustin blurted and dashed back

inside.

Barrett stormed back toward the house as angrily as he'd stormed to the porch.

My neighbor looked incredibly tiny standing in the dark on the front lawn. But as small and frail as she appeared, I knew there was more to her. She was strong inside, and I was sure one day she'd get the courage to get up and leave her horrid husband for a better life.

"Aimee—" I started to say, but she placed her little hand against my chest to stop me.

"It's all right. I'll be fine, James." She glanced toward my house. Barrett had already gone inside. "He was just doing what he thought was right. Don't be too hard on him."

I shook my head and grinned. "Believe me, I'm going to be on the receiving end of the tongue lashing. I broke a very important guy's rule tonight— never stop another guy from throwing his fist at someone. He'll get over it though." I looked down at the grass beneath my feet. "Do you need some help with that mower?"

She tucked her hair behind her tiny ears. She always wore the same tiny pearl earrings, and I always wondered if they had been a gift from Dustin. "The less time I spend inside, the better. I actually find it sort of relaxing."

"Good night then, Aimee."

"Good night, James."

Barrett had thrown on his motorcycle jacket and bound his long hair with a leather strap.

"Where are you going?"

He pulled his wallet out and looked briefly through it before shoving it back into his pocket. "Out," he answered without looking at me.

"Look, Barrett, I know you were trying to help, but Aimee has been with the guy for awhile. She looks fragile and pretty like a helpless kitten, but she knows how to take care of herself. And pissing off her husband doesn't make her life any easier. I think she'll leave him one day, but it's not our business." I thought about Aimee's words and how Barrett was just trying to do what was right. Sometimes my kid brother was more like me than I realized. "She was thankful though. She told me so."

He still hadn't looked me. "I'm going out. I'll be back later."

"Take the car. Your bike looks like it needs a major tune-up."

He shook his head. "It gets me where I'm going, and that's all I need."

I blocked the door as he headed to it. He finally looked up at me.

"Look, Rett, I'm sorry I stopped you from hitting the guy."

Rage flickered in his eyes. "Yeah, whatever. Now, can you move so I can leave?"

"Don't get wasted and ride that bike."

He reached for the doorknob. "Why don't you just worry about your life and let me worry about mine." I stepped aside. He flew out and slammed the door shut behind him.

***

Scotlyn was deep in concentration as I walked into the shop. I'd stayed up late watching mindless action movies, mostly because my head was still so wrapped around the moments with Taylor. It had only been seconds, but it had had huge impact. It had left me completely confused and pissed for giving in to something I'd denied myself forever and at completely the wrong time. Her reaction had been so mixed, I had no idea what to think. Typical for me when it came to women. In between thinking about Taylor, I'd wondered if Barrett would make it home alive. He'd left in a rage and on his wreck of a bike. Not a good combination. I'd finally fallen asleep on the couch when he crept back into the house. Without a word, he'd walked straight into the back bedroom.

The shop had just opened and there were no customers yet. "Hey, Scottie."

She lifted her hand to wave as I headed to the office.

I stopped. "Is Jason in back?"

She nodded.

"We're going to the bank at ten, so I'll need you to watch the place."

She flashed me a thumbs up.

Something was wrong. Scotlyn always reverted to hand gestures and facial expressions when she was upset. I walked over to her, but she didn't look up from the keyboard.

"What's the matter?"

She looked up questioningly, which only confirmed my suspicions.

"Come on, Scottie, you always get really quiet when you're upset. What happened?"

She bit her bottom lip. I was sure she wasn't going to tell

me but then she peeked quickly toward the office door. "It's nothing," she said. "Jason is mad at me."

"For what?"

She opened her mouth to speak just as Jason stepped into the room. He saw me and the serious expression on his face hardened more. He brushed past me to Scotlyn. "Look, Scotlyn, I'm sorry I got so angry. I know you were just trying to help by letting Taylor stay on the boat, but my parents are having a terrible time with her again—" Jason glanced back at me as if to say none of this was for my ears, but I shot him a look that assured him I wasn't going anywhere.

It was rare to see Scotlyn mad, and it was amazing how stunning she could look even in anger. "I think you should stop siding with your parents and take your sister's side for a change. Talk about being ganged up on— maybe your parents are being terrible."

"You don't understand, Scotlyn. Taylor has you charmed, that's all. She's really good at that. My parents just want her to stay out of trouble."

Scotlyn may have been silent when I walked in, but the gates had opened now. And I liked it. "Seems to me that she could have definitely gotten into trouble last night, but, instead, she got on a bus and came to the houseboat. We had cocoa and girl talk and then she slept on the couch. Doesn't sound too rebellious to me. And I talked her into calling your parents so they wouldn't worry. She's eighteen now. Next time I'll let *her* decide whether to call or not." Scotlyn returned to her keyboard, leaving Jason speechless. There wasn't much to argue. She'd been right. My stunned and silenced partner returned to the back room.

Scotlyn handed me a list of phone calls to make. I took my cue to get to work and headed to my desk. It was obvious Taylor had broken out of the mold Jason and his parents had made for her and, of course, I immediately wondered if it meant that her perfectly appropriate high school boyfriend was no longer in the picture. The way she'd kissed me back, for the brief seconds before remembering that she hated me, had been hot enough to let me believe that things weren't that terrific with the polished school boy.

I was in the middle of a phone call with a possible buyer for the Corvette I'd restored when I heard Barrett's distinctive laugh from the front room.

I finished the call and walked out of the office. Barrett was wearing his flashy white smile as he leaned over the counter chatting with Scotlyn.

"Hey, Bro," he called across the room brightly as if he hadn't left the house last night ready to kill me. Pretty girls had that effect on him. He was good at never letting them see his darker side . . .unless it worked in his favor.

"You're out and about early. Where are you headed?"

He lifted his hands. "What? Can't I just be out visiting my big brother?"

"Cut the shit, Rett. You're up about three hours earlier than usual."

He leaned one arm on the counter and managed to shoot off one more flirtatious grin at Scotlyn before looking back at me. "I was wondering if the old Chevy truck was running. I need to pick up a friend at the airport."

"It's running. What friend?"

He hesitated. "Gus, the guy I worked with on the fishing

boat."

"You mean the guy who got you high and then kicked off the boat?"

Beautiful girl standing nearby or not, some of the rage from the night before returned. "It wasn't as simple as all that. And besides, he thinks he's got a job for me on another boat."

"You rode all the way over here to ask me for the truck? Why didn't you just call?"

He snuck a peek at Scotlyn and then twisted his mouth as if he was deciding whether or not to answer. "I left my phone at a friend's house last night."

It was all quite clear now. "So you hooked up with some girl and you left your phone at her house?" I knew my brother too well. "And you snuck out without saying good-bye, and now you're stuck without a phone because you don't want to see her again."

Scotlyn pretended to busy herself with work, but she was holding back a smile.

"Jeez, Jimmy, you make me sound like a man-slut."

Scotlyn pressed her hand against her lips to suppress a laugh.

"I don't make you *sound* like one," I said. "You are one."

"Yeah, maybe I just like to have a good time. So can I borrow the truck or not?"

Jason walked out from the back with some boxes. "I'm going to ship these. I'll be back in time to go to the bank." He nodded at Barrett and walked out.

Seeing my partner made me realize that I was being just

as much an asshole to Barrett as Jason had been to his sister. I needed to lay off and let him make his own decisions, as stupid as they, no doubt, would be. "The keys are in the kitchen cupboard at home, but you'll owe me for gas. That truck gets about five miles per gallon."

My sudden change of tone shocked Barrett, and he stared at me for a second before gracing Scotlyn with another smile and leaving.

Scotlyn was still holding back a laugh as he hurried out. I was glad to see that her mood had lightened.

"Not you too," I said.

Her blue gaze lifted from the monitor. "Me too, what?"

"There isn't a female on this planet who doesn't find my kid brother adorable."

She glanced out the window as Barrett pulled away from the curb on his loud bike. "I'll bet the girl he snuck out on this morning doesn't think he's so adorable."

"Good point. And if she's smart, she is texting every girl in his phone list with some rude comment to piss them all off."

She nodded. "That sounds like an appropriate punishment. And, yes, to answer your question, he is adorable. There is something about him that reminds me of—"

"A stray puppy?" I finished for her.

She laughed. "Yes, I guess that's it."

CHAPTER 12

Taylor

I'd never been big on having a lot of close girlfriends growing up, but the two that I had spent most of my spare time with had basically threatened to shun me forever if I didn't meet them after school at the taco stand for a gossip session. I knew the only real gossip they were interested in was my break-up with Adam. Rumors had been swirling through the hallways all day— another one of a million reasons why I was anxious for high school to be over. But at the risk of not having anyone to eat lunch with, especially now that I was the *bitch* who broke Adam Gray's heart, I'd agreed to meet Jasmine and Kiley.

Unfortunately, it seemed that everyone else from high school had gotten the taco urge too. The senior class president had backed his truck up near the eating area, and his music was blasting over the wobbly fiberglass tables that were too hot to sit on in summer and cold on the butt in winter. Today had been perfectly warm, and, it seemed, half the student body had swarmed the place for cheap tacos. The owners never minded because they sold a crapload of tacos and cokes and most of the time there wasn't any trouble.

I shuffled past a repeat of the chorus line of cold glares that had followed me along the line of lockers that morning. Adam was greatly loved on campus, and overnight,

I had become the harsh witch who'd hurt him. He must have been spreading a massive sob story around campus to drum up sympathy from the bevy of girls who already worshipped him.

"Taylor!" Jasmine yelled to me from across the way. I walked over to her. She could have cared less if everyone was pissed at me. Not giving a shit about what other people thought was one of the reasons I'd stayed friends with her. Kiley was the opposite, but she'd obviously decided that hearing the juicy story of the break-up was worth a few scowls from her classmates. They'd saved me a spot at the small table that butted up to the parking lot. I scooted in between them.

Jasmine slid a soda in front of me. "We want to hear every detail so don't leave out a thing."

I took a long sip of the drink for dramatic effect as if I was about to divulge the juiciest break up story in the world. Then I swallowed and relaxed with a sigh. Jasmine and Kiley both stared hungrily at me as if I was a blueberry cheesecake. I took a breath. "Adam and I broke up."

Jasmine shifted on the bench anxiously. "Yeah, the entire school knows that but the details, Girl, the details. Was there a hideous fight? Did he catch you with someone else?"

My mouth dropped as I turned toward her. "Why do you assume that I would be the one cheating?"

She paused but only for a second. Jasmine was also brutally honest— another thing I liked about her. "Oh, come on, Taylor, out of the two of you, you would be the one to mess around. Not Adam."

She was right. It might have been one of the reasons behind me not falling madly and passionately in love with

Adam. He was too damn safe.

"I guess you're right." I tapped my chin. "Detail? Let me think. Well—"

They both leaned toward me.

"Well, we decided not to see each other anymore and then I got out of his car and I walked inside my house."

"Oh, come on," Kiley said disappointedly and probably regretting that she'd risked being seen with me for an uneventful break up story.

"Seriously, nothing exciting happened."

"But you broke up with him, right? What was your reason?" Jasmine was putting forth her best effort to make the story juicy even if it wasn't.

I shrugged. "It was sort of mutual, but I knew I was just dating him to please my parents. The guilt of it got to me."

Jasmine's shoulders slumped in disappointment. "That just sucks. And only you, my friend, would date the most popular guy in school to please your parents. Do you know how many girls have crushes on him?"

"I know. That's why I figured he'd get over it quickly." I glanced around. Most people had returned to their tacos and conversations, but there were still a few icy glares from the table of cheerleaders. "And you'd think girls would be thanking me for making him available again."

"I think the bad vibes are mostly Adam's doing," Kiley said. "They do love to protect their own at our silly little high school. I'm so done with it all."

I took a sip of my drink. "That makes two of us."

Jasmine picked up her cell phone. "I think I've gotten

one text all day, and it came from my mom so it doesn't even count. Speaking of moms," she said, and I knew what was coming next. "What's yours doing now that you broke it off with Adam? Or does she know?" She grabbed my arm. "You aren't going to be shipped off to Florida again, are you?"

"She's taking the break-up hard, almost as if she'd been dating Adam instead of me, but no, I'm not going back to my aunt's." Nix had dropped me off at my house before school. My parents were, of course, waiting with tight lips and flared nostrils. But I was ready for them. "I told my parents that if they wanted me to get a high school diploma, they had to leave me alone and let me finish school here. Otherwise, I'm not going to graduate." I'd formulated the threat while tossing and turning and fighting off seasickness on Nix's couch. I was sure they wouldn't go for it, so I had a plan B. I would leave home but this time I wouldn't chicken out. I'd stay gone for good. Surprisingly, my parents had agreed to my deal.

"So," Jasmine spoke up, "have you seen *him* yet?"

There were few people who didn't know about my obsession with Clutch, and I wished I'd been more discreet. But it had been too hard to hide. "I've seen him a few times," I said casually as if each time hadn't hit me like a high speed train. "But I'm moving on to new things. Clutch was my high school crush, and we're not suited for each other." Every word sounded like a laughable lie in my head, but I needed to persuade myself that I was done thinking about him.

Kylie elbowed me. "Speaking of Jimmy Mason, isn't that Barrett?"

A subtle hush had fallen over the crowd as Barrett walked through the maze of tables to the order window. Jason had told me he was back in town, but I hadn't seen him yet. He commanded his usual attention with his long blond hair, wide shoulders and Hollywood face. A tall, lanky guy with a mosaic of tattoos on both arms and long black hair was with him. He looked like a guy who'd been around the block more than once and quite possibly the block had been a jail block. Barrett always migrated toward the dark, edgy types as if he was always hoping trouble would find him. Which it often did.

Kiley nearly fell off the edge of the bench watching Barrett walk to the order window. "I was in total and complete mourning when that boy got expelled from school. There wasn't anything to wake up for and drag my ass to class knowing he was no longer going to grace the halls with his presence."

I looked over at her. "I didn't realize you had such a big thing for him."

She shot me a disgusted look. "That's because you were so absorbed with your own crush on his older brother, you never paid my wants and needs any attention."

I stared at her. "Wants and needs? God, you're dramatic. And, besides, if you wanted him so badly, why didn't you just go for it?"

"Because that would have been about as successful as your attempts to catch his brother." When Kiley's claws came out, they were always extra sharp.

"Damn," Jasmine gushed, "he's just as dreamy as ever." She looked over at me. "I thought he was out on a fishing boat somewhere."

"Yeah, I think he had a problem and came back home. I don't really know. Jason doesn't talk about stuff much."

Kiley drew a loud slurp through her straw. "Come to think of it, how come you never dated Barrett?" she asked.

"Because he's not Clutch," Jasmine answered for me, and she was right. I'd always gotten along well with Barrett. We were both the irritating younger siblings, but that had been our only common bond. And, Jasmine had phrased it perfectly, Barrett wasn't Clutch.

Kiley broke into a coughing fit as she sucked in a big sip. Barrett and his friend were headed to our table, once again we were drawing unwanted attention from the rest of the taco eaters.

Barrett smiled. Kiley and Jasmine stiffened next to me. "Hey, Tater Tot."

"I'd forgotten about that stupid nickname," I groaned. "I heard you were back, Rett. Couldn't hack it out on the fishing boat?" I hadn't seen him for awhile, but we'd always spent most of our time together harassing each other.

"I hacked it just fine, Tater Tot." He sat down and I was sure I heard Kiley suck in a breath. His friend scooted in across from us too. He was inked from his knuckles up to his neck.

Barrett lifted his chin toward Jasmine and Kiley. "Girls, how are you doing? This is my friend, Gus. We were out on the Bering Sea together."

"And what are your names?" Gus asked staring straight at me.

Jasmine shifted on her butt and straightened. "Yeah, Barrett, what are our names? Or do you even remember?"

"This is Taylor." Barrett lifted his sunglasses, and Kiley sucked in another breath. I was certain she would collapse into a dead faint if he so much as spoke to her. He squinted at Jasmine as if that would jog his memory. "Yeah, I remember you—" Barrett had no real reason to remember her name. She was three years younger and hadn't any contact with him except to drool over him along with the other freshmen girls. "You're that girl who always wore the jeans that were ripped along one thigh. Best pair of denims I've ever seen."

I could almost feel the heat of Jasmine's blush radiating from her skin. Her tough exterior melted, and she giggled in a fashion that I'd never heard from her. Barrett always knew exactly what to say. If only his brother had learned that skill.

Kiley reached across the table. "I'm Kiley." Amazingly, she'd managed to speak and even shake his hand without passing out.

He squinted again and pointed at her. "You used to have a bottom locker in the same row as me. It was always a pleasure watching you dig out your textbooks."

A tiny, shrill sound chirped from Kiley's mouth, and her hand flew to her lips to make sure nothing else escaped.

I looked at Barrett. "I see you haven't changed a bit." Aside from his incredible looks, it suddenly came back to me that he had an unsurpassed talent for winning people over, even if he didn't remember names.

Barrett's order number was called. He jumped up to pick up his food.

I looked over at Gus. "So, how long are you in town for?"

"Long enough, I hope." It was a strange answer.

"Long enough for what?"

"Long enough to get to know you." From anyone else it would have sounded like a well-practiced line, but there was something really intense and raw about Barrett's friend. He didn't seem like a guy who'd flirt or flatter without serious intentions, unlike his blond pal.

Barrett returned with their tacos. "Here you go, but I've got to warn you, it's not going to be like the fish you get up in Alaska. Nothing is that tasty."

"It seems like seafood would lose its appeal if you spent a lot of months on a fishing boat," I said.

Gus shrugged. "Sometimes. It kind of depends on who you share it with." He held up his taco. "Want a bite?" He was talking to me as if we were the only people at the table, and it was both weird and kind of cool all at the same time.

I leaned forward and took a bite of his taco. He watched my mouth with such scrutiny, I could feel my cheeks warm.

"So, Dray told me you were banished from seeing my brother?" Barrett blurted. The look he gave me told me that his interruption was well planned. "Although, knowing how you are, Tater Tot, you would go out of your way to see him just because you weren't supposed to. I guess that was how you got shipped off to Florida."

I picked up the soda. "Look who's talking." I shot a questioning look of why are you being such an ass, which he picked up on right away. It seemed that he sensed something between his friend and me, and he'd gone into brother loyalty mode. It was both tragic and amusing how so many people just assumed that Clutch and I would be together some day. I was slowly facing the ugly reality that it would never be. But the people who knew us best still hadn't come to that conclusion.

"You're right. It's none of my business." He focused on his tacos for a second and then must have decided to make my life his business again. "Wait a minute— were you at the car meet last night?"

I stared at him without responding.

He pointed at me with his taco. "I knew it. That would explain why Jimmy was in such a bad mood on the way home."

Jasmine snickered.

"Yeah, I saw him, and thanks for assuming that I was the one who put him in a bad mood. Maybe he was just annoyed because you were with him."

It must have been cryptic and confusing to Gus, but he listened to our conversation intently. "Clutch is Jimmy, your brother, right?" he finally asked for clarification. Then he turned to me. "Are you with Barrett's brother?"

Jasmine removed the top from her cup to get at the ice. "She wishes."

I scowled her way, and she quickly filled her mouth with ice and pretended she hadn't just made the bitchy remark.

"It's late. I've got to head home." The conversation was boring me. I stood from the table, and Gus's eyes followed me.

"Hey, are you going to Cassie and Dray's party tonight?" Barrett asked before I walked away.

"Scotlyn asked me to go with them but I'm not sure."

"Ah, come on," Barrett said, "you should come. I think Jimmy was picking up some car that he has been dying to get his hands on. He'll probably spend the whole night staring at his new purchase. I'll bet he won't even be there."

"I might go," I said. "It was nice meeting you, Gus." Amusingly, it occurred to me that I wanted Clutch to be there just as much as I didn't want him to show.

CHAPTER 13

Clutch

The little wreck of a glorious car looked so fragile, it seemed I could pick it up and crush it in my fist. I'd moved some of my weights and pushed it into my garage. I didn't trust the garage at the shop. The car, even in its immobile, rusty state, was too valuable. I threw the padlock on the garage door.

Aimee was just walking up her driveway. She waved to me and walked inside. Luckily, the incident with Barrett hadn't caused her any trouble, or at least any more trouble than she already had.

Barrett was still out with the truck, and I hadn't seen him all day. My phone buzzed and I pulled it out. It was Dray. "Nix said you weren't coming tonight because of your new car. That's bullshit, Dude. Cassie will be insulted if you don't show."

"That's because when I talked to Nix I hadn't heard what time I could pick her up. She's safe and sound in my garage now, so I'll be there."

"Good thing. I thought I might have to come over there and kick your ass."

I laughed. "Yeah, you and what army?"

"Seriously, you better show. Cassie invited that high school friend she wanted you to meet. She thinks you two would be perfect for each other."

I harrumphed into the phone. "I love Cassie and everything, but this desire to fix me up has got to end."

"Yeah, yeah, that's what I've been telling her. Just make sure you're there and that you smell nice. Later."

***

Barrett had not returned home. I had no idea what he was up to, but I was pretty sure it wasn't anything good. Halfway through my shower it had occurred to me that Taylor might show up at Dray's house. But from the conversation Jason had had with Scotlyn, it sounded as if Taylor was having more problems at home, which probably meant she wouldn't be out partying. My feelings about her were so confused I didn't know if I wanted her to be there or if I would be more relieved not to see her. It was like being stuck back in high school again. Something I didn't need.

There were already plenty of cars lined up along the street in front of Cassie and Dray's house. It was always interesting when the two mixed their extremely different friends into one party, but, surprisingly, it was always a good time. Two of the guys that I knew only as Dray's sparring partners sat on the front porch drinking beers and talking with two of Cassie's friends. They parted and I slid between them and through the open front door.

Cassie spotted me instantly, which was easy to do. I had to duck to walk beneath the ceiling fan that hung between their living room and dining room. I'd managed to crown myself on it enough times that I'd ended up with a small, permanent dent on my forehead.

"Oh good, you're here," she grabbed my hand and

dragged me toward the kitchen.

"Are Nix and Scottie here yet?" I asked as she motioned for me to bend down beneath the low kitchen doorway.

"Not yet." A girl, who could have been Cassie's taller twin, with dyed black hair, long bangs and several facial piercings, leaned against the kitchen counter sipping a fruity drink. Sparkling blue eyes smiled up at me from beneath the fringe of black bangs. There was a spray of tiny stars tattooed along her neck. As usual, my size produced the highly familiar stunned reaction, but she recovered quickly.

"Violet, this is Jimmy, the friend I told you about."

She put down her drink to shake my hand. "I figured it must be. I doubted you could have more than one friend who has to duck beneath doorways."

"Hey, Violet, nice to meet you. Cassie has told me a lot about you." The only thing I knew for sure about her was that she was just getting over a really bad break up with some guy she'd dated since high school. And the last thing I needed or wanted was to be someone's rebound guy. But sometimes Cassie was as pushy as Dray, only without the threats of violence.

Cassie handed me a beer and scurried out, obviously confident that she'd started something major in her tiny kitchen.

Violet picked up her drink again. Her nails were painted yellow, and I briefly wondered if her ex had gotten tired of the creepy colored nail polish. "Cass tells me you're into cars."

I smiled into my beer and nodded. I could never fig-ure out the exact meaning of being *into* something. "I restore classic cars and sell rare car parts. So, I guess I'm into them. They make me money, and I'm really into having shelter and food." I had no idea why I was being a dick, but she didn't seem to mind.

She nodded in agreement. "Money is good. I make custom jewelry." Her wrists and fingers were proof of that.

"That must be your jewelry in the display case at Freefall. It sells well."

"Yeah, Nix is such a doll. He lets Cassie use his shop as my storefront. He hasn't asked for any compensation. He is such a doll."

"Yeah, you mentioned that." If I had a dollar for every time I'd heard some girl call Nix a doll, I could stop being *into* cars and retire.

She reached over and grabbed the glass pitcher off the blender to refresh her drink. "My ex drives a sixty-nine Camaro."

Had to be a record. Only ten seconds into the conversation and we were on to the ex-boyfriend topic.

"That's a good car if it's done right."

"Oh, he did it right. Got a nice number of speeding tickets in it. One of the things we used to fight about." She waved the hand not holding the drink, and her bracelets jangled with the motion. "But you don't want hear about him. He's a jerk."

"I really don't. So, what do you do besides jewelry?" I hadn't meant it to be a leading question, but my poor grammar produced a wicked smile and she leaned toward me.

"It depends on just how much alcohol I've had." She lifted her drink to her mouth and stared at me over the brim as she sipped it down.

Of course, the other side of the rebound coin was the unfulfilled sex life due to the break up. "Is that right?" I asked. Lately, I'd been so wrapped up in my business and other people's lives, I'd ignored my own needs. Just maybe it was time to take care of those needs.

Dray's loud, distinctive laugh floated in through the open kitchen window. I looked out into the yard. He was handing Barrett a beer. I hadn't expected to see him but then it made sense that Dray would have invited the other pea from his pod. Aside from appearances, they sometimes seemed more like brothers than Barrett and me.

There was a real sketchy looking guy standing next to Barrett. It had to be the infamous Gus. He actually looked just as I'd expected, like one of the greasy haired dudes who'd hung out on the stoner's bench at school. Only this guy looked really hardcore.

Violet turned around to see what had gotten my attention. She turned back to face me. "That has to be your brother. He looks like a miniature version of you."

I nodded. "What's sad about that is that a guy who is six foot tall and a hundred and seventy pounds is mini compared to me."

She smiled and ran her long fingernail down my arm. "I do like big." She pressed her thigh against me. Then something behind me caught her attention and she smiled brightly. "Hey, Nix."

I turned around. Nix was standing in the small kitchen, but my attention was sucked away from him and the girl pressing her thigh against me. Taylor was standing with Scotlyn in the adjacent dining room. Our gazes met just long enough to punch the breath from me and then she headed out the back door.

I glowered down at Nix.

"Didn't you get my text?" he asked.

I pulled out my phone and read it. "We're bringing Taylor with us." I shoved it back in my pocket. "I've got it now." My pulse was pounding behind my ears and suddenly I wanted to be anywhere but here.

"She's already spotted you," Nix said.

"Really," I glanced around the small kitchen, "and I was sure no one would see me cloaked as I am in the kitchen walls. In fact, this whole damn place is starting to close in on me."

"Look, man, I'm sorry. Taylor has become really attached to Scotlyn. She feels like she doesn't have anyone else to turn to or trust. It's been good for Scotlyn too. She lost her sister. Taylor promised she wouldn't drink." He pointed at my pocket. "And I tried to warn you."

"Look, it's fine," I said tersely.

"Yeah, all right," Nix said. "I'm going out to get a beer." He nodded toward Violet and left.

"Who was that kid?" Violet asked, obviously sensing the tension that had built around me in the last few seconds.

"She's not a kid." And that's when it occurred to me— I had not admitted it out loud yet, which was probably out of self-preservation. All the months of thinking of Taylor as a kid had made it seem impossible to think that she was finally an adult. I'd denied myself the pleasure of looking at her, touching her and wanting her for so long that I'd built up a shield of self-control when it came to Taylor. When

I'd broken through that shield and kissed her, it had only caused her more confusion and hurt.

"She just looked kind of young to be here," Violet commented unnecessarily. She continued to ramble on about something, but I didn't hear a word. My attention had been drawn to the scene outside the window where Taylor had immediately walked up to Barrett and Gus. She was talking animatedly to Barrett's shady-looking buddy as if they already knew each other.

Violet poked my arm. "Did you hear me?"

I dragged my gaze away from the window and looked down at her. "Huh?"

"Never mind," she said angrily, "I don't need this shit. I'm going out to the yard." I stepped obligingly aside, and she brushed past me.

I stared out the window and watched Taylor. She'd made it clear she would have rather seen anyone but me tonight. And maybe it was better if I didn't see her. I could head back home and drink down a few more and sit in the garage staring at the Shelby. I'd always gotten along better with cars than girls.

Taylor laughed and lifted up her ankle to show the tiny butterfly Nix had drawn for her. Barrett's slimy fishing mate reached down and brushed his fingers over it. I flew out the back door with enough force that half the yard turned around. But she hadn't turned or looked away from her new friend. I somehow managed to stop myself from walking over and pounding the guy into the ground.

I leaned up against the brick wall pretending I could hide in the corner of the yard. A party was going on around me, but I was focused solely on her. Thick copper strands of hair bounced off her tanned shoulders framing the birth-mark that started just below the strap of her tank shirt and ended just above her elbow. It was a subtle difference in skin color that few people would ever notice, but I'd mem-orized everything about her. Like the fact that she had only one dimple, which showed prominently as she tucked her hair behind her ear and laughed at something that Barrett's friend had said. It had been months since I'd heard her laugh, but everything about it was familiar.

If she had seen me standing in the shadowy edge of the yard, she hadn't let on, or maybe, she just didn't give a damn that I was there. A half-filled ice chest slid across the cement and stopped directly in front of me. I stared down at it.

"Something told me you should be closer to the beer—" Dray glanced over at Taylor, "—for all our sakes." He seemed to be assessing whether or not it was safe to get near me, which was completely out of character for my friend who never thought twice about walking into a brawl with three guys twice his size. He finally walked over and plucked a beer out of the ice chest. "Just a warning—Cassie's already upset with you."

I downed the rest of my beer and crushed the can before tossing it into the ice chest. "Don't seem to be able to make anyone happy these days. Maybe it will put a quick end to her matchmaker profession."

Dray lifted his can in the air. "Here, here."

Nix walked over and grabbed a can of beer. "It figures you two would be hovering over the ice chest." He glanced across the yard too. "Who the hell is that guy with Barrett?"

"The son of the fishing boat captain, and the guy who

got him hooked on drugs," I answered.

"I've got to hand it to your brother, he's consistent. I don't know anyone else who manages to always form friendships with the worst people on the planet," Nix said.

Dray gulped back a mouthful. "Hey, I take offense to that. Barrett and I are friends."

"Fine, I take it back. But it doesn't necessarily disprove my point."

Taylor threw her head back with another laugh, and I felt the sound of it deep inside my chest. Then Gus reached over and placed his arm around her waist. It had only been for a split second. If I had blinked, I would have missed it. But I hadn't blinked.

Nix's hand was on my arm before I could take one step. "Let it go. If you care about her, which I know you do, then let it go. You need to kick back and take a breath."

"Yeah, chill out," Dray said. "I don't want to have to scrape that greasy scumbag off my patio. Taylor's probably just messing with your head. She might be young, but she knows damn well what she's doing."

I nodded but every muscle in my body was taut. "I don't think I'll be able to hang out here for too much longer. To think I was only worried about this guy's arrival for Barrett's sake," I said with a short laugh.

Scotlyn and Cassie walked by with most of the women, including her friend, Violet, who managed to shoot me a snarly look over her shoulder before disappearing inside. Taylor stayed outside with Barrett and Gus. My brother was doing a great job at pretending I was nowhere around, but he knew damn well I was standing just yards from him.

In fact, I was sure he was acutely aware of my proximity.

"We're going in to have cheese fondue," Cassie called from the stoop. "You guys can stick with chips and salsa. We girls prefer finer fare."

Dray held out his hands. "I like cheese, as long as there is macaroni in it."

"Then you're out of luck. We're dipping in raw vegetables," Cassie answered.

"Who the hell dips raw vegetables in cheese?" Dray motioned for her to go inside. He looked back at us. "For that matter, who the fuck eats raw vegetables at all, except for rabbits . . . and chicks, I guess."

Nix motioned with his head toward the small, bricked-in patio at the east end of the yard. "Speaking of chips and salsa, who are those guys with the biker jackets sitting at the table?" "They're some of my buddies from the docks. Thought I'd throw a few longshoremen into the mix."

"Well, it looks like you have mixed things up too much," Nix said. "It looks like some of your sparring partners aren't taking too kindly to them hogging the snacks."

Dray laughed it off. "What can I say? They're all a bunch of hot heads."

My focus went back to the only thing at the party that held my interest. Barrett and Gus's attention had been drawn away from Taylor by a fighter, who Dray had nick-named Granite because he'd noted that hitting his face was like hitting rock. I had never heard the guy's real name, but his neck was as thick as his giant block-shaped head. And his nose resembled a head of cauliflower.

My head stood up above everyone's. I was hard to avoid

and with no one to talk to, it seemed Taylor had finally given up pretending that she hadn't noticed me. Cassie had hung decorative lanterns around the patio, and the wavering light they produced cast an uneven glow over the yard. But we locked gazes and stared at each other as if the other people had all disappeared. Even in the unsteady light and even from the distance I stood, I could see the flicker of anger and hurt in her face. I didn't know how to fix it. For two years, the girl had followed me around. No matter where I was, I could count on her to find me or text me or call me. Now I'd managed to push her away just as I'd come to the realization that I needed her near me. She dragged her gaze from mine, and it felt as if she'd pulled physically away from me.

Without warning, the bowl of chips went flying across the yard and hit one of Dray's workmates on the back of the head. He swung around with tight fists just as Granite swung a fist at Gus. The guy was wiry enough to duck out of the way, but before I could take one step, a wild, fist flying brawl broke out. Taylor stood in the center like a little girl standing in the middle of a traffic-filled road just waiting to be struck.

"Sonavabitch," Dray growled, "I'm not going to hear the end of this from Cassie." As he spoke, the back door flew open and Scotlyn and Cassie raced out.

Nix grabbed Scotlyn around the waist. "Go back inside. We'll take care of this."

Scotlyn struggled to free herself. "Get Taylor out—"

I was across the yard in three strides. Taylor's arms were wrapped around Granite's thick neck, and she dangled from his shoulders like a kid's backpack. The jerk managed

119

to plow his fist into Barrett's stomach before I could stop him. My brother dropped to his knees, doubled over and gasping for air. Taylor swung her long legs out and kicked the back of the guy's calves. He reached back to pluck her off his neck, but I grabbed her first.

The chaos continued at full jaw cracking, furniture breaking pace around us as I pulled Taylor against me. I held her under one arm and glanced around for Nix. I pointed to Barrett who was still gasping for air. "Nix, drag his ass out of there before someone hits him again."

Taylor kicked and pounded her fists on me as I threw her over my shoulder and carried her toward the house. She grabbed hold of the doorway to stop me from getting inside. "Let me go!" she screamed. Her fists flailed wildly in her struggle to get free, and she managed to smack my back.

My grip on her tightened. "Dammit, Taylor." I placed her down hard on her feet in the center of the kitchen. Cassie and her friends were enjoying the male circus of testosterone from the window. A few of them were still snacking on fondue while they watched in half-terror and half-amusement.

Taylor tried to dash past me, but my arm shot out and caught her. "Fucking hell, Taylor, you know sometimes it's all right to step away from trouble instead of flying head first into it."

"I was trying to help your brother," she cried and pounded my chest with her fists.

I took hold of her wrists. "Barrett can take care of himself."

She wrenched herself free from my grasp. The rage in

her expression felt like someone had punched me in the stomach. We stared hard at each other, and it seemed that the spectators in the kitchen had grown bored of the scene outside and had shifted their focus to the anger-filled scene in the center of the kitchen.

"I didn't want you to get hurt," I said.

She met my comment with the Taylor chin lift, a gesture that pissed me off as much as it made me want to kiss the pout off her lips. "I can take care of myself."

My laugh echoed off the walls. Another huge mistake. "Really? You thought you could hold your own in the fray with trained fighters, longshoremen and a fucking deep sea fisherman?"

The tension between us had silenced the small audience, and the only sounds were the grunts and yells outside and a few carrots being nibbled.

Then, without warning, tears formed in Taylor's eyes. I'd managed to make her cry twice in the same week. My skill at being an asshole seemed to have no bounds.

"After all this time, don't bother to pretend that I matter to you now." She stormed out of the kitchen and out the front door. Scotlyn followed her.

I looked briefly around at the faces in the kitchen. The harshest glare came from Cassie's friend, Violet. I was obviously the villain in the little drama that had just played out. I decided to take my chances with the trained fighters and dock workers.

Nix and Dray were standing at the edge of the fight. Barrett was sitting along the short retaining wall that separated the patio from the grass. Several others sat next to him nursing their injuries with cold beer cans.

I looked down at Dray. "This seems like your kind of party game. Why are you just standing here?"

"Well, naturally I would love to be in there beating in a few skulls, but I can't be on either side of the match without pissing off my fight buddies or my work buddies."

Nix looked over at me. "It's quite the conundrum."

Dray looked up at him. "Conundrum?"

"Cool word, huh?" Nix said. "This little librarian was in my shop today trying to decide whether to have an Edgar Allan Poe or a Mark Twain quote tattooed on her shoulder. She called it a *conundrum* and I've been waiting for a chance to use the word. Perfect opportunity."

"I'm impressed," I said.

Cassie walked up next to us with her camera poised. "Darn, this light sucks. I'm missing some great shots." She moved closer just as a large body came stumbling backwards. With amazing reflexes, Dray hooked her around the waist and pulled her out of the way. She hardly noticed that she'd almost been slammed to the ground. Without missing a beat, she stepped back toward the action.

"Plunging right into the war zone," I said. "She really is a professional."

Dray tried to act nonchalant, but he didn't take his eyes off of her. "I just hope she gets some good pictures. Then maybe I won't have to sleep on the couch tonight."

The brawlers seemed to be losing steam, but a few of the tougher guys were sticking it out, including Barrett's friend. Blood was dripping from his mouth and one eye looked swollen, but he was still swinging.

"I've got to say, Barrett's friend has more in him than I'd have thought," Dray said.

Nix laughed. "Hell yeah, you put any of these other guys out on that Bering Sea for a day, and they'd all be crying for their mommies."

"He's probably just too high to feel any pain," I said angrily.

Dray's friend, Granite, took one to his gut and flew backward, taking the string of decorative lanterns with him. They shattered on the patio.

Cassie swung around. "Now I'm pissed. Do something, Dray."

"Damn, I guess it's going to be the couch after all," Dray trudged over to the table and climbed on top of it. His loud whistle split the air. "Fight's over. We've had a patio ornament casualty." The action slowed and then stopped. Most seemed more than happy to end it, with the exception of Gus who took one last swing at an unsuspecting victim. The cheap shot nearly started the fight again, and, this time, it looked as if it would be everyone against the fisherman. Dray looked over at Barrett. "Get that asshole out of here now before I jump down there and take him out myself."

Barrett got up. "Let's go, Gus. Party's over." It seemed as if every fist in the yard was still clenched, including my own, until Gus and Barrett had left out the back gate.

Dray hopped down and walked back over to Nix and me. "Guess I'm going to have to clean up this mess."

"I'm certainly not doing it," Cassie said sharply as she walked past.

"Well," I said with a sigh, "it's been one helluva party. I

blew off a horny girl who had a thing for big men. I managed to make Taylor hate me even more. And my brother just left with a sleazebag who not only looks like he just broke out of prison, but looks as if he murdered the prison guards with his bare hands to escape. All in all, not the best night."

Dray grinned up at me. "You forgot the part about Taylor seeming to have a thing for the guy."

"Yeah, thanks. I was hoping that part was just my imagination." I looked over at Nix. "Where was that bridge nicknamed Suicide Bridge? Was it Pasadena?"

Nix placed his hand on my shoulder. "Things aren't that bad. Don't forget about the Shelby."

"That's right. At least I've got the Shelby."

CHAPTER 14

Taylor

I slid my backpack onto my shoulders. I'd packed plenty of textbooks inside to make it look extra studious. "Mom," I called from the entryway, "I'm going to wait out front for Kiley and then we're off to the library."

Mom stepped out of the family room and glanced at my shorts. "You don't look very dressed for the library." We'd been going through this every day. She'd question everything suspiciously, and I'd answer with all the confidence of a practiced liar, which, unfortunately, I was. And my intuition told me that my mom knew I was lying about everything but that she'd sort of given up on trying catching me at stuff.

I glanced down at my shorts and sandals. "I didn't realize the public library had a dress code."

"They don't, but they should," she said curtly. "You sure are wearing a lot of perfume."

I'd showered and sprayed it on without thinking, but I wasn't ready to let my guard down. Sometimes it seemed these little interrogation sessions were meant to break me, but I held firmly to my web of bullshit. "Maybe we should add perfume to my list of no-nos. I mean who knows what kind of shenanigans I could get into wearing perfume."

Her lips drew tight. She hated my sarcastic tongue more

than my *potty* mouth. She sighed loudly. "*You* certainly don't need perfume to get into shenanigans. Speaking of no-nos, you've been staying away from Jimmy, right?"

I didn't answer.

Her neatly plucked brow arched. "Taylor?"

"It's a little hard to stay clear of him when we hang out with a lot of the same people. After all, he is Jason's best friend and partner. I don't know why you hate him so much all of a sudden."

"Don't be so dramatic, Taylor. Of course I don't hate him. It's just that he is a man and you're—" she paused, wisely reconsidering her words. She walked up to me and buttoned the top button on my shirt. "It's just that I know you've always had a crush on him, and sometimes a crush can cause a girl to make bad decisions. Jimmy is a grown man with a grown man's needs."

It was all I could do to keep from laughing. "Mom, we aren't seriously having the birds and bees discussion." It was a conversation my mom had always been to prudish to have with me. "Because you're five years too late. I learned everything from my friends in seventh grade."

She bit her lip to show that she wasn't shocked by anything I had to say.

The woman was delusional, and sometimes, she needed a dose of reality. "You don't actually think that Adam and I were just holding hands when we were sitting out there in his car?"

She looked up at me with wide eyes. A horn blew outside.

"There's Kiley. Later, Mom." It was time to end our conversation. I left her standing speechless and shocked in the entryway. For the longest time I'd felt guilt about causing her so much grief, but sometimes it seemed that I'd turned out the way I had just because she'd tried to keep me in her unrealistic *everything is cotton candy and marshmallow* bubble.

I threw my backpack into the backseat and slid into the passenger seat. "Holy crap, you got here just in time." I pulled down the visor and checked my make-up in the mirror.

Kiley didn't say anything as she pulled abruptly away from the curb.

I looked over at her. "What's wrong?"

She lifted her shoulder. "Nothing, but I think this is the end of our bargain. I don't like being the middle man in your tawdry double life. And I don't think you should be hanging around with that guy anyway. He's pure trouble."

"I've told you we're just friends. He knows I'm not into him like that. He's different and he likes to have fun. I held up my end of the bargain and set you up on a date with Barrett. You owe me a few more escapes."

She looked over the front seat to my backpack. "I can't believe your mom actually thinks you're out studying. I just know she's going to catch you and then I'm going to be caught up in all this shit." She turned up the radio. "Besides, Barrett never called me after our date."

I nodded. "Oh, that's what this is all about. Hey, my end of the bargain was to set you up with him. I can't be responsible for how things turned out. I warned you that the boy was a player. I've never seen Barrett Mason hook up with any girl for longer than a month."

We turned the corner, and the shabby car that Gus had borrowed from his mom was parked beneath the giant oak tree at the far end of the park. Sometimes I couldn't even explain my decisions to myself. Maybe I was doing this just for attention like my mom always insisted, even though my parents were the last people in the world I wanted or needed attention from. Maybe it was out of complete and utter boredom that I always found myself going down the worst possible path. Or maybe since Clutch insisted that I always flew head first into trouble, I'd decided to prove him right.

Gus had been in town for two weeks, and he'd spent most of that time with me. And I'd gone back and forth with my feelings about him. One minute it felt wrong and even sleazy to be hanging out with him, and the next minute I felt as if I could live in the dark, edgy world he drifted in. He was completely fearless, and he treated me like I was worth something. Not like I was some little girl who liked to get in trouble. I'd made it clear to him that I was only interested in friendship, and even though he'd kissed me a few times, he hadn't really tried anything.

Kiley snorted in disgust as we pulled into the spot next to him. "He's a total scumbag, and if you're trying to make James Mason jealous, you're wasting your time. And what's worse, if you're using him like you did Adam, then watch out. He looks like a guy who could get pretty damn dangerous if he's pissed off."

Her words stung and gave me pause at the same time. But I was getting tired of people lecturing me about my actions. I reached over the seat for my backpack. "You know what— forget our deal. It's not worth it. A conversation with you is like a conversation with my mom but without the prospect of home baked cookies afterward." I opened the car door and jumped out. "Thanks for the ride."

I slid into a cloud of pot smoke and rolled down the window. "I just got questioned about wearing perfume. The last thing I need is to smell like weed."

Gus leaned over and kissed my cheek and then stopped to smell my neck. "I like the perfume better." Kiley's words replayed in my head. I'd been living with the guilt of what I'd done to Adam, and I promised myself I would never do anything like that again. I'd done it out of desperation. I wanted to stay in California.

As much as I hadn't really been into the perfect, shiny type like Adam, this guy was on the whole other side of the spectrum. I'd been bored and I was desperate to forget about Clutch. I'd been desperate to prove to myself that I could stop being so crazy about him. But Kiley was wrong. I hadn't been hanging out with Gus to make Clutch jealous. Clutch had no idea I'd been out with him, or at least that was what Barrett had told me. I'd sworn Barrett to secrecy, and he'd assured me that he would be in just as much deep shit as me if Clutch or Jason ever found out. I was hanging out with Gus because he'd come to California to visit his mom and he wanted someone to hang with. Gus had lived with his mother in Los Angeles after his parent's divorce five years ago. But then his father offered him a job on his boat, and he'd left the warm sunshine behind for the ice covered plains and mountains of Alaska. It was too much money to pass up he'd told me. Knowing that Barrett was living back in California, Gus had made the trip figuring he'd have someone to hang out with. And Barrett, who had the attention span of six week old puppy, had basically abandoned the guy. I liked being with him. He was totally different than anyone else and I loved hearing his outrageous stories about Alaska and the Bering Sea.

Gus's eyes were red, but he'd washed and combed his hair. Somehow, the fresh and clean look just didn't work for him. "I thought we'd get something to eat and then go watch some drag races Barrett told me about. I might even make a wager or two and earn some cash." He started up the car. "You look gorgeous, by the way. If you ever came up to Alaska, the guys would go crazy. We're definitely short on *gorgeous* up there." He smacked his steering wheel. "Brilliant idea." He glanced over at me and then pulled out of the parking lot. "If your parents try to ship you off again or kick you out of the house, you should move up there. There are tons of jobs and the wages are high."

"And the snow is thick," I said. I'd laid out my whole sordid list of family problems one day while we ate lunch on the beach. Something I regretted now.

"True, but it's beautiful up there. Lots of adventure." He winked at me, but I was fairly certain we were on different pages when it came to adventure.

"I don't do snow," I said. "I went snowboarding a couple of times, but I spent less time on my feet and more time freezing my butt off on the ice. I'm a hot, sunny California girl down to the core."

"You'd be surprised how quickly you get used to it." He glanced over at me. "What do you say, Sweets? Shall we go to watch some cars race?"

If Barrett had known about the race then it was possible that Clutch was there. My cover would be blown.

Gus smiled enthusiastically. "I'm in the mood for some gambling."

The crowd was always thick at the races, and I had the advantage. Clutch always towered over everyone else and he was easy to spot. I could easily avoid him if I was vigilant. "I guess we could go to the races." A knot formed in my stomach as I agreed.

"Ooh, an In N Out." Gus looked at me. "Do you mind if we eat there? They don't have any in Juneau, and I've been craving a double-double for months."

"No problem." I'd been hungry when I slid into the car, but my appetite had vanished with the drag racing suggestion.

As usual, the line snaked around the block. Gus's car rumbled unsteadily as we inched forward toward the order window.

"You know there are tons of 'hair on fire' adventures in Alaska. You can go rafting."

I shrugged. "Colorado River and it's not dotted with chunks of ice."

"There's kayaking. I've got a great picture of me in a kayak on my cell phone." He reached for his phone, and the car inched forward and nearly bumped into the fender in front of us.

I held up my hand. "Show me another time and pay attention to the *road*. Besides, there are plenty of places to kayak in California."

He waved his finger at me. "Dog sledding and the northern lights." He knew he had me on those.

I laughed. "Are you secretly employed by the Alaska Visitor's Bureau?"

"It's a habit. When I meet an incredible, beautiful, fun

girl, I try to coax her to move up north. We're short on women up there."

"Oh really. And how many women has it worked on so far?"

"Zero. You're the first one I've tried my sales pitch on, and you don't seem convinced."

We pulled up to the window and Gus looked at me. "I just want pink lemonade."

He shook his head. "What is it with you women? Pink lemonade is hardly a dinner."

Gus downed his hamburger in record time, and we headed to the races. Raspy sounding music squeaked out of the speakers in the back. "I'll have to text Barrett when we get there and find out where the bookie hangs out." He smiled over at me. "I guess Barrett will know who to place a wager on too. He mentioned that his brother was racing tonight."

I stiffened in my seat. Jason had told me that Clutch had gotten in to the amateur drag racing circuit, but I'd been hoping these races had nothing to do with him.

"Is he fast?"

I hadn't expected the question, and I stumbled over an answer. "He-he always has one of the best cars, but I don't know anything else." The last thing I wanted to do was talk to Gus about Clutch.

"Well, I'll have to grill Barrett when we get there. I don't like to lose."

The nerves in my stomach twisted tighter.

Thankfully, the race track was packed with spectators. It would be much easier to stay camouflaged. I fell purposely behind as Gus walked toward the concession stands where

Barrett was waiting for us. He was sitting at a small table beneath an umbrella talking to two girls when we walked up. It was obvious from the look he gave me that he hadn't expected me to be with Gus. The two girls sneered at me as I slid onto the bench next to Barrett.

Barrett lifted his phone. "I'll call you tomorrow," he said to the petite brunette. Begrudgingly, they left the table but not without scowling at me once more.

"I'll call you tomorrow," I repeated in my best Barrett imitation. "Maybe."

Barrett looked over at me. "You don't know. I might call her."

Gus sat down across from him. He leaned forward. "So who do I see to place a bet, and who should I lay some money on? Is your brother fast?"

"He won the last time he was out here, so I guess he's fast." Barrett took out his phone. "Let me find out where the bookie is at, but he only deals in cash with strangers . . . especially ones who are from out of state."

"Clutch won last time?" I asked, trying to mask my interest with a casual tone.

Barrett faced me again, and that sliver of a cocky grin that he was so good at appeared. "Why, yes he did." He looked down at the table then. "I wasn't there though. I'd just gotten into town."

"I can't believe you made it all the way from Alaska without any—"

Barrett's blue eyes flashed angrily at Gus, and he stopped midsentence.

Barrett felt my scrutiny on the side of his face. I'd heard

that he'd been in some kind of trouble up north, but Jason had never told me any details. I wasn't even completely sure that Jason knew. Clutch was not the kind to blab stuff around.

Barrett combed his hair back with his fingers and nodded. "Yeah, it wasn't a great trip." The faraway sadness in his tone assured me that he'd been through something shitty. His phone buzzed and he read the text. "The dude's name is Oscar, and he's over by the stands. You can't miss him. He's got a long, mountain man style beard, and he is usually wearing a black shirt with a dollar sign on it."

Gus got up from the bench, and Barrett casually drummed a beat on the table. The second Gus had disappeared into the crowd, he grabbed my arm. "What the fuck are you doing here, Taylor?"

I pulled my arm from his grasp. "I was out with Gus, and you're the idiot who told him about the races."

"Yeah, and I specifically told him not to bring you because you hated the drag races. Jimmy is over in the pits, and he'll have my head when he finds out that you are hanging with Gus. He'll have your pretty head too." He combed his hair back again. "Not to mention that Jason will string me up from the rafters. It took my brother a week to convince him to let me work at the shop, and now I'm going to be looking for a job again all because of you."

I smacked him hard on the shoulder. "Up yours, you ass. Don't blame me for your problems."

"Do you know how hard it's been lying to them both all week when they asked about Gus?"

"I wouldn't think it had been hard at all for a professional bullshitter like yourself. And, frankly, what I do is none of your brother's business."

"Yeah, right. Tell him that. I can't believe you hooked up with Gus."

"We haven't *hooked* up. I'm not you. I don't fall into bed with every living, breathing person I meet." I stared down and rubbed my fingertips over the names and words that had been carved into the plastic table top. "He's fun to hang out with that's all." My gaze shot back up to him. "And I felt bad for him because you've been avoiding him, and he doesn't have a lot of friends down here."

"There's a reason I've been avoiding him. He's a bad influence on me. He might seem like a really cool guy, but the dude is into all kinds of shit. And he has a terrible temper. Remember Dray's party?"

"He's been really mellow around me. I don't see the problem."

"Yeah, well, you wouldn't." His attention was momentarily drawn away by two passing girls in tight jeans and then he looked back at me. "You still have a lot of growing up to do."

"Ooh, you're such an ass tonight." I stood from the table and glanced around for Gus. "Anyhow, Gus is leaving soon, and my cover was Kiley," I glared down at him, "who you pissed off with your usual *I'll call you* promise. I plan on telling Gus later on that I'm not going to be able to hang out with him anymore."

He shook his head. "I never promised Kiley that I'd call her. I didn't realize that I was part of your evil plan." Barrett stood from the table. "Tater Tot, you sure know how to cause problems."

"Like you're a saint or something. I'll just stay clear of Clutch. He's easy to spot even in a crowd like this."

Barrett shook his head and dropped his heavy arm around my shoulder. "Tater, Tater, Tater." He looked down at me. "I just realized something."

"What's that?"

"It has been years since I've given you a proper noogie." Before I could react or withdraw from his arm, his knuckles came up on my head. But then he stopped and pulled out his phone. "Saved by a text." He read the message. "Jimmy wants a bottle of water. I'll see you later." He slid his arm off my shoulder and turned to leave but then stopped and smiled back at me. "And try to stay out of trouble."

"Yeah, you too. And stop promising girls you'll call them, you cad."

CHAPTER 15

Clutch

I downed the water bottle in one long series of gulps. "You could have bought me the bigger size, Cheapskate. It's hot tonight, and there's no breeze at all."

Barrett had been uncharacteristically silent while he waited with me for my race. He looked around a few times as if he was worried about running into someone.

"Who are you looking for?" And then it dawned on me. "Shit, Rett, did you hit on some guy's girlfriend out here? One of these days you're going to pick up on the wrong girl and—"

"Stop, jeez, sometimes you drone on like Dad used to whenever I failed a test. And I didn't hit on any girls, at least none that were attached to someone."

I walked around to inspect the tires for a second time just to be sure. I'd felt off all night as if I shouldn't race. I'd managed to laugh off the feeling until now, yet somehow, Barrett's nervous demeanor had made me feeling even less confident. But the Chevelle had been running tight, and there weren't that many serious, hardcore racers in the mix tonight. Once again, I pushed the uneasiness down into my gut. It was the last thing I needed and the surest way for things to go awry.

Rowdy, the event organizer, walked over. "You're up

next. You're going up against Stanton in the Nova."

I nodded and Rowdy walked away.

"Is that good or bad?' Barrett asked.

"I like the car but hate the driver. He's a blowhard, but it's not like we're going out on a date." I rubbed a tingling sensation out of the back of my neck.

"What's wrong? You don't seem that thrilled to be here tonight."

"Yeah, I guess I'm not in the mood to race tonight. I should have just stayed home, but too late now."

Barrett leaned against the side of the car and checked his phone.

"Expecting someone?" I asked.

His face shot up, and he nearly dropped his phone. "No. Why?"

"Hell, you're as skittish as a rabbit in a wolf's den tonight. I thought you mentioned something about Gus coming, that's all."

He put away the phone. "Nope. Not expectin' anyone."

Rowdy waved which was my cue to head to the staging area. I rolled down the window. "See you at the finish line, Rett."

I rolled into the staging area and gave the dashboard a hearty pat for luck. The motor rumbled beneath me like a gigantic purring cat, and my earlier apprehension had vanished. "Here we go, Sweetheart. Let's win this again."

The seventy Nova reached the staging area too. The tires were watered, and the smell of burning rubber filled the air. I stared at the lights on the tree, and the familiar rush of adrenaline coursed through me. Then something caught my eye. It was just a flicker of movement in a sea of people, but my gaze was drawn to it like a magnet. Taylor was standing in the crowd with Barrett's friend.

Tires screeched. The light had gone green, and I'd missed it. Without thinking, I overcompensated by slamming my foot treacherously hard on the pedal. I moved only ten feet and the tires shook. Before I could let off the gas, the rear end fishtailed. The crowd blurred as I spun toward the guardrail and braced myself for the impact. For a second, it felt almost as if I was flying and then my journey came to an abrupt, jarring end. Everything went black.

My eyes opened and it took me several seconds to remember that I'd just been in a wreck. I took several deep breaths to force air back into my lungs. My ribs ached as they pushed against the seatbelt, and oddly, I found my mind drifting to the story Nix had told me about his father's crash and death. But the pain and the noise outside the car assured me I was still alive.

I moved both my feet and my hands. My limbs were still working which was comforting to know. My neck, head and back felt stiff with pain. The interior of the car was still mostly intact, but the custom driver's seat was leaning at an odd angle.

I squinted through the windshield and grimaced from the pain it caused my skull. At least a dozen people came running toward me, including the two stand-by medics with a gurney bouncing along behind them. Barrett's blond head was out in front and he got to me first. His face was as pale as the first night he'd arrived home sick and strung out.

He yanked open the car door and just over his shoulder,

I saw her. Her beautiful face was tight with worry. The seconds before the race were coming clearly back to me. One of the other drivers held onto her waist, and she pounded his arm as she tried to get past him. Her persistence paid off, and she broke into the inner circle of the wreck. Unable to get past the medics and the gurney, she stopped and froze in one spot looking a shade paler than Rett.

One of the medics put a blood pressure cuff around my arm before I even got out of the driver's seat. Every movement pained me. "Rett, how bad is it?"

He looked down at me. "Not too bad. Everything is still attached, and I don't see any blood except for that scratch on your forehead."

"Not me. The car. How does she look?"

Barrett leaned back and looked at the exterior of the car before bending down to me. "She's history. In fact, looking at this car, it's hard to tell that it was a Chevelle. What happened out there?"

I glanced over the heads to where Taylor stood like a stunning but ghostly pale mannequin in a store. She stared back at me, and like always, it felt as if she'd reached right into my chest and touched my heart. "I got distracted."

Barrett glanced back to see what had my attention. He hesitated as he turned back to face me. "Yeah, that was my fault."

"It usually is." I shifted my legs out of the car and groaned. Deep pain thudded through my muscles. "Bring her over here. She looks like she's about to faint."

The medics pushed everyone else out of the way and helped me to the gurney. Every inch of my body hurt as if

I'd been trapped on a roller coaster ride for a month, but I could tell there was nothing much wrong with me. "I don't really need this. My brother's here, and he can drive me to the emergency room."

"Sorry, these are Rowdy's rules."

I stretched out on the gurney, and my legs hung off the end. The width of it was short by several inches on each side. I looked up at the medic, who looked to be about Barrett's age. He looked a little panicked about having to get me into the ambulance. "I guess you forgot to bring your custom made gurney for giants." The gurney wobbled beneath my weight, and the rush of pain in my chest assured me that a couple of ribs had been bruised or cracked. Barrett returned to me, and I turned my head to look past him. My neck was feeling every bit of the impact.

Taylor wasn't with him. "Where is she?"

Barrett shook his head. "She was kind of freaked out. She ran off."

"But she must have seen me walk to the gurney."

Barrett looked away as if he was suddenly interested in the scenery. I called this his avoidance move. It was what he resorted to when he wanted to avoid telling me something.

"Rett, no fucking games tonight. It's been a shitty evening, and I just lost my best car."

He stared down at his feet like a kid about to get royally chewed out. "I sort of let it slip that you'd seen her and that that was when you crashed. I don't know what I was thinking."

"You're such an idiot." My phone had survived the

crash, and with effort, I pulled it out of my pocket to answer it. "Hey, Nix, I'm sort of busy—"

"Holy shit, Jimmy, thank God. Are you all right? I just saw the picture of your car." It was unusual enough to hear him call me by my real name, but his voice cracked as if he'd been close to crying.

"The picture?" I glanced up, and my brother looked off into the horizon again. "I'm fine, Nix. They'll take me in to get checked out. It's the rules. I'll call you after I see the doctor."

"Do you want me to meet you at the emergency room?"

"Not necessary. I've got Knucklehead with me, and he's got the truck."

"What happened? Did a tire blow?" His tone had stabilized.

I sighed and my ribs ached from the release of air. "No, it wasn't the tires." I thought briefly about my reaction at seeing Taylor. Two years ago, the kid with ridiculously long legs, an addiction to lip gloss and a penchant for trouble had worked her way into my head and heart and damn if she wasn't still tied tightly to both. "They're going to slide me into the ambulance now. I'll call you later."

"Take care, Buddy." His breathing had finally slowed.

Barrett could have sent the same picture to my dad and he probably would have called and asked why the hell I'd destroyed an expensive car. It was like that with Nix and Dray. Growing up, and even now, we'd always had each other's backs because no one else did.

Barrett hovered nearby with his hands deep in his pockets looking sheepish and dodging direct eye contact. The medics started to push the gurney. "Hey guys, hold on a second. Rett, come over here."

He walked over. Not all the color had returned to his face yet. I lifted my hand and motioned him closer with my fingers. He leaned down. "I'm glad you're here, Bro," I said quietly and honestly. Then I slapped the back of his head like I used to do whenever he did something stupid. "Idiot."

He straightened and rubbed the back of his head. "I guess I should've written a text with the picture letting Nix know you were all right."

"You think?" I took one last look at my beloved Chevelle. The next time I was feeling off before a race, I was definitely staying home. "Go ahead," I told the medics.

***

An hour into the pain pills, it was easy to understand how people became addicted to them. I'd felt like shit in the examination room and during the x-rays on my rib cage and my knee that had swollen to the size of a grapefruit during the ambulance ride. Nothing had been broken, at least not any bones.

Removing my shirt and shoes was about all the effort I could put into getting ready for bed. My bedroom looked strangely smaller as I stretched out on my mattress and enjoyed the blissful numbness that had started as a haze in my aching head and had since flowed down to my feet. My knee throbbed as the skin rubbed against the rough material of my jeans, but after the crash I'd just lived through, I had no real right to feel as good as I did. Rowdy had had the Chevelle towed to the shop, but I was sure even the parts wouldn't be worth much.

I had no patience to flip through the hundreds of channels on television. I lifted the remote and switched it off. The only light and sound was coming from the front room where Barrett was watching a movie. He'd hardly talked the entire ride home, and I'd probably been too hard on him. He had witnessed his brother crashing into a guardrail just minutes before making two stunningly stupid decisions. He'd had no real excuse for telling Taylor that she'd distracted me just before the race except that she'd asked him what had happened and it was the first response that had fallen out of his mouth. He'd pout about it for a day or two, but he got over things quickly.

My door opened and Barrett walked in with a glass of water. He lowered it onto my nightstand. "For the pain meds because I know what a wuss you are about swallowing. Plus, that type of pill gives you cotton mouth."

"Spoken like a true expert. I was wondering if I should hide the bottles." I regretted the comment instantly. His face dropped. "I'm kidding, Rett. It's the pills talking. Thanks for driving me home."

He nodded.

"Hey, how long has Taylor been hanging out with that scumbag?"

The avoidance move made a third appearance for the evening. Barrett glanced at the floor as if he was checking out the carpeting. "I'm not completely sure. It's not any big deal. I'd stopped hanging with him—" he reached for the prescription bottles on my nightstand, shoved them inside and shut the drawer. "Gus is too much temptation. The guy loves to get high. He's a good salesman, and I'm a fucking pushover."

"Great, and Taylor's hanging out with him." I was quickly regretting starting this conversation. My head was already pounding.

"Taylor has never liked any of that shit. When he's not over-the top wasted, the guy is pretty interesting to be around. He's seen a lot of the world, and he has one of the most dangerous jobs. Chicks love that."

"Yeah, that's just fucking awesome." I pressed my arm against my rib cage. It felt as if I'd scrambled the bones around and put them back in the wrong place. Breathing regularly was a chore.

"Uh, considering how Taylor reacted tonight when she witnessed the accident, I don't think you have too much to worry about."

There was a knock at the front door. "You expecting someone?" I asked.

"Not me. Don't get up. I'll go see who it is."

"I think it would take a crane to get me off this bed."

Barrett left the room. My eyelids felt heavy and my eyes drifted shut. I was on the edge of a deep, drug-laced sleep when soft breathing pulled me back. My mind was in a fog, but I knew whose lips the breath had floated from. Even after the night I'd had, I knew who was standing in my room before I opened my eyes.

I turned my head. The light from the living room framed her breath-stealing silhouette and then my eyes focused enough to see her face clearly in the faint light. The paleness had gone, but shock and distress still marred her amazing face.

"Don't look like that, Taylor. None of this was your fault."

Tears welled up in her eyes. "Barrett said—"

"Since when do you listen to anything Rett says? Really, I'm fine, and these painkillers are fucking awesome."

She smiled beneath the stream of tears. She stood there for a long silent minute and then she walked across the room, slipped off her sandals and lifted the covers. My heart pounded against my sore ribs as she slid under the blankets and tucked herself in next to me.

Her sweet smelling warmth was even more comforting than the drugs as I cradled her against my sore ribs. She pressed her face against my chest.

So much had happened in the space of one evening, and my head was spinning from all of it. But nothing was more significant than this moment, holding Taylor, the woman I loved, in my arms.

She snuggled next to me, and her familiar fragrance filled my senses, senses that were heightened by the drugs and by having her so damn close.

She lifted her face and looked up at me. "By the way, this doesn't change anything. I still hate you."

I pulled her closer and had to restrain myself from holding her too tightly. "Yeah, I know."

CHAPTER 16

Taylor

My phone buzzed in my pocket waking me from a sound sleep. Lying tucked against Clutch's hard chest with his massive arms around me felt just as I'd expected, safe, comforting and right. I was meant to be this close to him always but crazy stuff always seemed to get in the way. And, as much as I knew this was the place I was supposed to be, he seemed completely unsure. Tonight, when I'd seen his car fly into the guardrail, I'd grabbed Gus's arm to keep from falling to my knees. As soon as I'd felt steady enough to run, I jammed through the crowd to get to him, terrified of what I might find when I got there. More than once, Jason had told me the tragic story of how Nix watched his dad die in a car race, and that horrifying scenario flashed through my mind as I ran to him.

Relief had washed over me as I saw him emerge from his car and walk to the gurney, but when Barrett had let it slip that he'd seen me in the crowd with Gus just before the race, the horror returned. Gus had dropped me back off at the park to wait for a ride that I knew wasn't ever coming. Once his car was out of sight, I walked to the nearest bus stop. I had to see Clutch. I had to know that he was all right.

Clutch took a deep breath, and his chest pressed harder against my cheek. I could hear the steady, slow beat of his heart. The pain medication had dropped him into a deep sleep. My phone buzzed again with urgency. I managed to free an arm and reach into my pocket.

"You should get home now," Jason's text read. It was amazing how much command and threat my brother could put into five words.

I slid the phone back into my pocket and looked up at Clutch's face. He was breathtaking even in sleep. I scooted up and his arms instinctively tightened around me as if he had no intention of letting me slip away. If only that were the case. If only he knew that all he had to do was ask and I would stay with him forever. I kissed his lips lightly and he stirred but didn't wake.

I managed to free myself from his grasp. I slipped on my sandals and tiptoed out of the room. Barrett was stretched out on the couch with his arm hanging on the ground and his hand still wrapped around a beer. He was fast asleep.

I crept across the room, hoping I hadn't missed the midnight bus or I'd be even later getting home. At this point, I just didn't give a shit what my parents had to say about me being out late.

"Let me give you a ride home, Tater," a groggy voice floated up from the couch.

"I'll just take the bus."

Barrett sat up and combed his long hair back with his fingers. He squinted into the light of the room. "Nah, it's late. All kinds of mass murderers ride those buses at this hour."

"All kinds? I didn't know there was a variety of them out there."

He reached for his shoes and put them on. "Hell yeah,

there is." He pushed up from the couch and reached into his pocket for keys. He reached the door and smiled down at me with those blue eyes that were his strongest weapon. "And they all love to prey on pretty girls with copper hair and pouty lips."

"Oh?" We walked outside. I hugged myself against the drastic drop in temperature from being wrapped in Clutch's giant arms to the cool, clear spring night. "How do you know they don't like pretty boys with blond hair?"

He scowled down at me. "You know I hate being called pretty."

"That is why I chose that particular adjective." I walked over to the passenger side. "But, hey, thanks for the lift. From the text I just received from Jason, it seems a fun therapy and intervention session is waiting for me at home." I climbed inside the cab and realized that my load was a little light. "Damn it, I left my backpack in the back of Gus's car. I guess I've just blown my out late studying cover."

Barrett looked over at me as he stuck the key in the ignition. "Seriously? Your parents thought *you* were out studying?"

"Hey, I study."

His laughter filled the truck cab as he backed out of the driveway.

I reached forward and messed with the radio until something decent came on. "He's going to really feel this tomorrow," I said quietly into the blaring music.

"Yep, it's always worse the next day." Barrett glanced over at me. "Thanks for coming to see him tonight. I'm sure it made him feel better."

"He was so drugged up, I doubt he'll even remember I was there."

He laughed again, but it had a completely different sound. "Believe me, he'll remember it. Don't worry about your backpack. I'll get it back from Gus. I know you were going to tell him that you couldn't hang out with him anymore. How'd he take it?"

I stared silently out the passenger window.

"You didn't tell him, did you?"

I shrugged. "So much happened tonight, I just didn't have the strength to do it. But I will. Besides, he's leaving in two weeks and then he'll be thousands of miles away."

"Coward."

"Right, I'm a coward. How many girls have you dated or gone home with that you've never called again?" I held up my hand. "Don't bother to try and count. The ride home isn't that long."

My street was dark and quiet as the truck puttered along between the neatly trimmed lawns. The cement sidewalks glowed beneath a nearly full moon. Barrett turned off the headlights several houses before mine. "Just in case your dad's got a shotgun sitting across his lap while he's perched rigid in his recliner waiting for his little troublemaker to come home."

"Thanks for that charming scenario. Like my heart isn't already beating fast enough."

His eyes widened and worry crossed his face. "He doesn't really have a gun, does he?" He grabbed my wrist. "He wouldn't hurt you, right?"

His concern was cute and something I'd rarely seen

from him. "No, he wouldn't unless you count yelling at me at the top of his lungs. That does hurt my ears some." I reached for the door and then smiled back at him. "You know I always think of you as just this good-looking guy who doesn't have much deep in here." I touched his chest. "There's hope for you yet, Barrett Mason." I leaned over and kissed his cheek. "Thanks for the ride back to the Dungeon of Doom."

My fingers trembled some as I pushed the key into the door. The only light on was the dim light Mom left on in the kitchen in case someone needed a glass of milk in the middle of the night. She'd always insisted it was for safety, but I was pretty sure it was so no one would spill anything on her glistening counters.

The house was eerily quiet as I crept down the long hallway to my bedroom. I would have almost preferred to have them meet me head on in the entryway or the kitchen. My heart was jumping around in my chest and I was bracing for a surprise attack. The flickering light coming from beneath their door let me know they were still up watching television. I passed their room and the light turned off. The only sound in the house was my grandmother's old mantle clock, the icemaker in the refrigerator and the pulse pounding in my ears.

I reached my door and slid inside. If I was going to face them, I preferred it to be on my own territory, especially because the mess in my room would probably distract my mom from the lecture. I washed my face and changed into the long t-shirt I always wore to bed. The wait was killing me. I just wanted to get it all over with. I had every intention of telling them everything. I was growing tired of making up stories and lies.

I climbed into bed and sat up against the bed board, watching for the door knob to turn like in one of those horror movies where the girl hears footsteps and then waits for the door to open. But there were no footsteps, only terrifying silence. All kinds of weird scenarios floated through my imagination, like waking up in the morning and finding myself strapped into the seat of an airplane headed to Florida. Or maybe they'd just put locks on the outside of the door and cut a slit to slide food into me. An unsettling quiet pervaded every corner of the house.

I leaned my head back and shut my eyes trying to relive the feeling of being wrapped in Clutch's arms. I would have given anything to be back there pressed against him, his soft snores ruffling the hair on the top of my head. My phone buzzed from the pocket of the shorts I'd thrown on the floor. I lunged for it as if the low vibration could be heard throughout the house.

I glanced at the screen, and my heart flipped around in my chest again but for a completely different reason. I'd called him hundreds of times, but I could count his phone calls on one hand.

"Hey," I said quietly. Every sound disturbed the stillness of the house.

There was a long pause and for a moment I thought he would hang up. "I woke up and you weren't there." I could sense that he was in physical pain.

"I needed to get home."

"I can't sleep."

"Take another pill."

"The only painkiller I need is you lying next to me."

I smiled and closed my eyes absorbing the words even though I knew they were probably a result of the drugs. "You're high."

He grew silent and I wondered if he'd drifted back off to sleep. "I'm not high. I want you, Taylor, here, next to me. Fuck what everyone else thinks. I need you."

"I know you do, you jerk." My throat tightened and it was hard to talk. "I've been trying to tell you that for two years."

I could hear his breathing through the phone, and I shut my eyes again and imagined it caressing my mouth before he kissed me.

"Do you still hate me?"

Unexpected tears rolled down my cheeks. This man certainly had a knack for making me cry. "Yes, I do."

"Are you crying?"

"No— yes— maybe." I wiped my tears away with the sleeve of my t-shirt.

"Taylor," he said quietly, "I never stop thinking about you." His labored breaths stuttered through the phone. "I've never stopped." I heard his bed squeak and he groaned in pain. My tears flowed faster.

My voice caught in my throat and I swallowed and took a deep breath. It was the pills talking, and I had to keep my head. "Hey, Viking, stop being so stoic and take a damn pill."

"I will," he finally said. "But I'm still not going to sleep without you pressed against me."

"Good night, Clutch."

CHAPTER 17

Clutch

Barrett looked up from his bowl of cereal. "There's no way you're going in today. You look like— like you were in a car crash." He smiled at his stupid comment and lifted the bowl to drink the milk.

The distance to the coffee pot seemed daunting. What normally took me three long strides across the floor turned into seven painstaking shuffles. My knee throbbed with every step but favoring the other leg sent a stab of pain through my back.

Barrett laughed as he lowered the bowl. "Holy shit, you look just like Grandpa Mason. I still remember when he would come to visit and he'd take those little mini steps, and if you got stuck behind him in the hallway, you had to wait like thirty minutes to get to the other end."

Pouring coffee took some effort. I turned around in slow motion and slid out a chair. The legs of the chair creaked as my knee gave out halfway down and I plopped down hard on the seat. I looked across the table at Barrett. "Jackass." I took a sip of coffee and nearly spit it out. "Who the hell taught you how to make coffee? It tastes like tar."

"That's how we made it on the boat, thick and black just like the cowboys used to drink it."

"Push the milk this way, Wild Bill. Maybe I can still

save my cup."

Barrett slid the milk carton toward me, and I drowned the coffee with milk. "Thanks for taking Taylor home last night." I'd woken to the lingering fragrance of her perfume on my sheets, and all I could think was that I wanted her to still be there my wrapped within my arms, pressing her sweet, seductive body against me. It would have definitely given me incentive to stay in bed instead of ignoring the painful protest from every muscle in my body.

"Crazy Tater Tot, she came here by bus, and she was actually planning to climb back on the bus to go home."

I stared down at the foamy mixture of coffee and milk. "Tater Tot, I haven't heard that nickname in a long time." My chest felt heavy, not as much from the drugs and the entire =wipeout of a night, but from missing her. She'd climbed silently into bed next to me, and it'd felt completely right. She belonged there. She'd always belonged there. There was no one else. Just Taylor.

Barrett got up to put his bowl in the sink. "Yeah, she doesn't really fit the nickname anymore, but old habits die hard. Are you really going in to work today?"

"Yeah, I've got stuff to do. Besides, I feel better if I'm moving around. Once I lay down, it is that much harder to peel my sorry ass out of bed. But you can drive me. Somehow sitting behind the wheel just doesn't sound fun today."

"Aren't you supposed to get back on the horse?"

"Not if that horse is going to be trotting through traffic on the L.A. freeways. And my head feels like it's filled with cotton today."

Barrett returned the milk to the refrigerator. "That

sounds like the perfect state of mind for sitting in traffic. Well, hurry up then, Grandpa. My boss is a real asshole when I'm late."

***

Barrett had managed to find every pothole and rough patch in the road and then seemed to take pleasure in hitting the driveway edge extra hard as he pulled in behind the shop. "Christ, is this how you treat my truck every day, or are you just in the mood to torture me?"

"Hey, this is how you taught me to drive, big brother."

I shook my head. "I'm not taking credit for your shitty ass driving."

"This coming from the man who left most of his Chevelle on the guardrail last night." The smirk on his face definitely needed to be wiped off, but I wasn't in the mood.

"Technically, that was your fault too." I glanced down at my phone for the hundredth time since we'd left the house. The summer before, I could count on her texting me or calling me at least three times a day. And, even though I'd acted annoyed, I hadn't been. It was stupid, but I was sure she would text me just to see how I was feeling.

"You must be expecting a very important call."

"Yep, and that's why I'm the boss. I get important calls." After sitting in the car for half an hour, climbing out hurt every muscle in my body.

"Or maybe you were just expecting a text from a certain long legged, sweet smelling girl."

I glanced over the top of the truck at him. "Shit, Rett, do I really need this crap today?"

"You're right. Sorry about that. I'm going inside to finish cleaning those parts. I'll let Scottie know that you'll be inside in—" He looked across the asphalt to the back door of the shop and then back at me. "In about twenty minutes." Once again pleased with his own humor, he laughed and headed to the door.

Scotlyn looked up from the computer. "Clutch!" She slid out from behind the counter and I noticed the tears just before she threw her arms around me. "Thank God you're all right."

I hugged her back. She was trembling slightly. "Hey, Scottie, I'm fine. Just a little sore. Sorry for giving you such a scare."

She lifted her face. "Don't do it again."

"Considering I had to put down my best horse, I don't think that'll be a problem."

She wiped a tear off her cheek with her thumb. "Your *horse* is in the garage, and after seeing it, I'm glad I wasn't there last night." She stepped back and looked at me. "I can't believe you're not hurt more."

"Just a badly swollen knee. Not sure what I hit it on, but that's my main complaint. I guess it helps to be built like a Viking."

She smiled weakly and patted my arm. "It's like having your own muscular suit of armor. Now go sit in your office and put that leg up. You shouldn't be standing on that knee. Jason isn't here yet, but I'm sure he can do deliveries today. I sent you some emails for part requests."

"I owe Jason one. He came in last night and opened up the shop for the tow truck." I limped to the office and fell into my chair. I was hopeful that Jason had had no clue about Taylor being at the race or with me after the race.

Scotlyn came in and slid the extra chair across the room and patted the seat cushion. "Put your leg up here, and I'll get you some coffee."

She left the office. The back door opened and slammed shut.

"I saw Barrett's truck out back," Jason's angry voice filled the front room. "Where is he?"

"He's out cleaning parts," Scotlyn answered hesitantly, assuring me that I hadn't misheard the rage in Jason's tone.

His footsteps pounded the tile floor of the shop, and I heard the door to the parts room creak as it swung open. "You fucking little weasel," Jason yelled.

I shot out of my chair, temporarily forgetting that everything hurt. I remembered the second my foot slammed on the ground. I grabbed my knee to stop the pulsating pain and then limped to the back room.

Barrett was standing looking completely shell shocked but with his fists ready for defense.

"You fucking loser. I let you work in my shop, and you hook my sister up with one of those lowlife, drugged-out friends of yours?" Jason stepped toward him.

"It's *our* shop," I said.

Jason swung around and his eyes popped open. "Clutch, I didn't think you were here."

"The way you just spoke to my brother, that's pretty fucking obvious."

He fell silent.

"What the hell, Jason? Have you lost your goddamned mind?" I asked.

My comment seemed to kick him back into offense mode. "This loser fixed Taylor up with—"

Apparently anger was a far better pain killer than opiates. I was in front of him before he could blink and my proximity shut him up fast. "Jason," I said between clenched teeth, and my tone drained the blood from his face. "We have been friends a long time, but if you call my brother a loser again, or anything else for that matter, I will knock you through that back wall."

He stretched up taller, something he always did when he was pissed at me. His head still barely reached my shoulder. "I'm just looking out for my little sister, just like you're looking out for him."

"Yeah, I get that, but your sister makes her own decisions. You should stop trying to control her." It was the first time I'd defended Taylor to her brother, and it made me realize what an asshole I'd been. I'd always been on his side and from the look on his face he was just as shocked as I was.

"I think you should mind your own damn business." He slid past me but then stopped. "And *you* stay the fuck away from her too. My parents are thinking of sending her off again, and it will be his fault." He pointed at Barrett and then spun back to face me. "And yours."

"Really?" He was not going to pull a cowardly retreat after that. "Because I think it's your parent's fault. And you're just as much to blame as them."

Jason's shoulders stiffened and he stopped in the doorway and looked back at me. He was pissed but so was I.

We'd argued plenty of times, but this was different. We were causing irreparable damage to our friendship and partnership.

"You selfish asshole, you have only one stake in this fight. You want my sister. Well, you're not going to have her. My parents will send her out of the fucking country if they have to."

"You are just your parent's whipping boy. And your girlfriend's too. And thanks for letting me know how you and your parents really feel about me. Funny that I'm good enough to be your business partner. Or is that just because I know how to make money?"

His mouth twisted as he seemed to consider his next words carefully. Shit had already hit the fan and sprayed the entire room. I doubted there was much more he could say to make things worse.

"My parents want better for Taylor. Let's just say they were hoping for someone from a *better* side of the tracks."

I'd been wrong. There was more shit to fling, and this was the worst crap of all.

Jason fidgeted as I stared down at him. For a second, it actually looked as if he wished he could suck the words back in, but it was way too late for that.

"Not that I give a fuck but good to know their opinion of me, *Partner.* All I know is that if ignorant people like your parents come from the *better* side of the tracks, then I'm glad to be from the *other* side."

With nothing else to say, he left the room. I turned back to Barrett, who still looked as stunned as a kid who'd stuck a paperclip in an electric socket.

I ran my hair back with my fingers and sighed as I glanced around at the piles of parts. Jason and I had started an awesome business together and it had already made way more money than either of us had expected, but this partnership grew more and more tenuous each day. Even so, it wasn't the business that weighed heavily on my chest. It was the girl.

CHAPTER 18

Taylor

Four seagulls were perched on the white marina fence staring hungrily through the windshield as Scotlyn parked the car. She laughed. "I think they know we have food."

We climbed out of the car, instinctively tucking our bucket of chicken and box of cookies beneath our coats for protection. An energetic coastal breeze had pushed the fog off the shore, and a full moon hovered low in the early night sky. "This was a great idea, Scottie. I'm really glad you invited me out here for dinner."

"Actually, I tried to call you last week, but you've been hard to reach. I know you were out at the races last Saturday when Clutch crashed, and I figured you had a pretty good scare. I'm so glad I wasn't there. Those races are terrifying to me."

"I can tell you that after last week's race, they are terrifying to me too. Sorry you couldn't reach me. I got home late that night and was sure my parents would lock me in my room for a year. Nothing happened that night, but I went to bed with that creeping feeling you get when you're sure something wicked is about to happen. I woke up the next morning and they'd taken away my phone and computer."

Scotlyn gasped. "You mean you had to go cold turkey without technology."

We reached the dock. The temperature dropped, and I held the chicken bucket tightly for warmth. "Yep. I told them they might was well lock me in a padded cell because I was going to be bouncing off the walls without my phone. They weren't amused. They are truly a lovely pair. . . and so rational with all their decisions. I wasn't supposed to go anywhere except school and home, but I reminded them that even though they took my electronics, they hadn't taken my feet. So, off I went. It was pretty darn funny because I could stay out late and my mom couldn't call to check up on me. It was driving her crazy, and I knew she badly wanted to give me the phone back."

Scotlyn shook her head with amusement. She pulled two cookies out of the box and handed me one. "I personally know the world would be an altogether better place if dessert came before every meal."

I bit the cookie. "I've been trying to convince my mom of that for years."

The breeze grew stronger as we got farther out over the water. Small navy blue waves splashed up against the hulls of the anchored boats. "How did you get your phone back?"

I smiled to myself. "It was all rather diabolical on my part, but I had been without technology for a week. Unless, of course, you count the primitive computers in the school lab where any site that is worth visiting has been blocked. I was eating breakfast before school on Friday, and I told my mom that the day before a freshman girl had been standing at the bus stop and some scary looking guy had jumped out of a van and tried to grab her. I told her she got away and quickly called the police on her cell phone." I finished the cookie and wiped the crumbs off my coat. "I could see the wheels of terror spinning and the reels of murderous scenarios turning in her head the whole time that I was reciting my completely bullshit story." My chuckle had an edge of guilt. "I picked up my backpack and kissed her on the cheek. She was behind me with my phone before I could take one step outside."

Scotlyn smiled over at me. "You're right, diabolical but probably necessary for her to come to her senses."

The Zany Lucy bobbed up and down and side to side in the rambunctious tide. We stepped on board. There was a 'for sale' sign in the kitchen window. "What? You guys are selling the Lucy?"

"I'm afraid so," Scotlyn said as she unlocked the cabin door. "She just needs too much work, and we don't have enough money for the upkeep."

We stepped inside and immediately I felt a bit queasy from the close surroundings and movement beneath my feet. "Can we eat outside? I think that cookie might make a reappearance if I stay in here too long."

"I'll grab some blankets. See, living on a boat does have some pitfalls," she said as she ducked into the bedroom. She reemerged with an armful of blankets. "I mean it can be lovely and incredibly romantic when all the elements are cooperating. But that is rare. The ocean has a mind of its own."

I took hold of one of the blankets. "Gus has told me some really scary stories about his time out on the Bering Sea."

Scotlyn was good at not verbally passing judgment, but her facial expressions always let you know what she was thinking.

"I'm not really seeing him," I said quickly. "He just picked me up a few times this week from school and we hung out." I had never gotten up the courage to say anything to Gus. I figured he was leaving soon and that would be the end of it.

We tucked ourselves onto the cushioned bench at the bow. We pulled the blankets over our shoulders and huddled for warmth. The deck rose and fell beneath our bottoms.

Scotlyn opened the chicken bucket. "Are you feeling better?"

"Yeah, it's always better out here in the open." I took a bite. "I've only heard little pieces of information about Clutch. How is he feeling?" I'd been dying to ask her about him all afternoon, but I hadn't wanted to seem overanxious. I'd acted silly as a desperate school girl for a long time, and I was determined to prove to everyone that I'd grown up. Of course, I still allowed myself the goofy pleasure of doodling his name all over my school notebooks. But no one else had to see that. And my doodles had definitely intensified since the night he'd called me. Even though it was obvious that he'd only called me because he was high and his words had been the drugs talking, I'd allowed myself the delusion of thinking that he'd meant them.

Scotlyn picked out a piece of chicken. "He's fine. He has still been limping some and he has been pressing his arm against his ribs as if they pain him a lot, but I think he's been much more distraught about losing that car." Salty moisture drifted up off the water and we both shivered. Scotlyn tugged the corners of the blanket shut under her chin. "You know, I think he tried to reach you a few times, but just like me, he didn't know that your phone had been taken."

I looked up from my drumstick. "Really?" I had to force back the excitement in my tone. "I'm sure that my brother knew that my phone was gone. He and my parents spend a great deal of their waking hours discussing all the things I've done wrong. It would have been nice for him to have let other people know I didn't have a phone." I dropped the chicken bone into my napkin and leaned against the back of the bench. "I guess he would never have mentioned it to Clutch since I'm not supposed to be talking to him."

Scotlyn reached for another piece of chicken and then decided not to take one. It seemed as if she had something she wanted to say, something that was distressing her, but she had a tendency to fall quiet when something upset her. She leaned back next to me and stared up at the sky.

I turned my head and looked at her. "There's something you haven't told me." Not that I was sure I wanted to hear it, but her sudden silence made me curious.

She pulled her blanket tighter and wriggled uncomfortably for a second. "Your brother and Clutch aren't talking at the moment."

I sat forward. "Really? I had no idea. Jeez, the crap that goes on when you have no connection to the world. What happened?"

Scotlyn stared down at her hands and twisted the corners of the blanket between her fingers. When other people fell silent it was just quiet, but when Scotlyn fell silent a huge amount of energy sucked in behind the quiet. But she really didn't need to say another word.

I leaned back and huddled beneath my blanket. The full moon reflected an amazing amount of light out over the water. "It was about me."

She didn't answer, which solidified my assumption.

"That's just great." I lunged forward and snatched up the box of cookies.

Scotlyn reached in the box for a cookie. "Look on the bright side. You've got so many people that love you, they're all fighting over you."

Scotlyn had no family except the one person who adored her enough for a whole family's worth of love and that was Nix. And, stupidly, I sort of envied her lack of ties to the world. Less hassle all around. "Yeah, I'm the lucky one all right."

The deck of the boat rose and fell, and my stomach dropped as if I was standing in an elevator. "I can see where the unsteady tide might make life aboard a little unsettling."

"See. I think I'm looking forward to a house with a foundation beneath it. Then the only thing I have to worry about is earthquakes." Scotlyn nibbled her cookie. "So, what are you planning to do once you graduate?"

The question had gone through my head hundreds of times, and I still hadn't come up with a coherent answer. Sort of like the rest of my life, it was muddled. "In my perfect future, I'm studying fashion design, but I'm sure my vision of utopia is far different from my parent's vision. I won't have the grades for a four year college. I have only myself to blame for that though. Of course, if I reached for it, I could probably find some hidden repressed memory of something lame my parents did that caused my lack of ambition at school."

"I could totally see you in fashion. You have this amazing sense of style that I've always envied. Like that cute little corset style top you're wearing tonight. I never would have thought about pairing something like that with a flouncy skirt and short boots but it's perfect."

"Thanks. I made this top myself. I love to sew. My mom says I'm way too daring with my ensembles but I say tough shit. I wear what I like." I drew the blanket over my bare legs. "But I must admit, this particular fashion statement isn't all that practical out on a boat."

"You are truly talented if you sewed that yourself. If you're cold, we could go inside," Scotlyn suggested.

"No, I love it out here on the water. Clears all the stuff out of my head that needs clearing. And lately, there's been a lot of stuff." I huddled closer to her. "So, what about you, Scotlyn? I know your earlier life took some really bad turns, but do you ever think about what you might want to do in the future?"

She paused for a second. "I'm going to start city college in the fall. I want to go into nursing."

"Wow, that's a tough profession. Good for you."

She gazed out at the water. There were times when she was impossibly pretty, like no one else I'd ever met in person. "After the accident, I was alone in the world. It was like this horrible black hole had swallowed me. While the doctors and social workers and my awful aunt stood around trying to figure out why I'd stopped talking and what my grim future held, the nurses were there comforting me. I could see my own despair mirrored in their expressions whenever they came in to take my temperature or bring my food tray. Nurse Frannie was so cool, she actually came into visit me on her off hours. I want to be like that. I want to be there for some kid who needs it too."

"I feel a little shallow now with my fashion designer dreams," I said.

She hugged me and laughed. "Shallow? I've never met anyone with more depth than you, Taylor Flinn."

We stayed cuddled together until loud footsteps on the dock made us turn. Nix hopped on deck with a twelve pack of beer under his arm. He hadn't seen us tucked beneath the blankets in the dark. Scotlyn lifted her finger to her lips telling me to keep quiet. Nix leaned down to unlock the cabin.

"I guess you're planning on getting plenty drunk tonight, huh sailor?" Nix straightened at the sound of Scotlyn's voice.

"I didn't see you sitting there." Then he noticed me, and his mouth dropped open. "Hey, Taylor." He glanced back down the dock and then back at me.

Scotlyn laughed. "Who are you expecting? Your secret lover?"

More footsteps pounded the wooden planks of the dock. Big footsteps, giant footsteps. The Zany Lucy tilted to the side slightly as he climbed on board.

The strangest sensation always surrounded me when I stood near him as if suddenly everything else around us had been sucked away and we were completely alone standing on some empty, desolate place, just the two of us, staring at each other, with sparks of heated energy flying between us, connecting us as much as pushing us away from each other. And always when I was near him, I could sense waves of tension flowing from him as if my presence caused him pain in some way. But this time was different. His shoulders were relaxed. His strong jaw wasn't twitching. His fingers weren't curled into fists. The only sign of tension was in his throat as his Adam's apple moved up and down.

"We were thinking about going down to the beach for a bonfire," Nix's voice broke through the quiet.

I looked over at Nix.

"Can you stay, Taylor?"

I turned back to Clutch. He hadn't taken his eyes off of me. "Do you want me to stay?"

At times, I forgot how massively built he was until I stood directly in front of him. His eyes looked pale and intense in the dim light. "What do you think?"

CHAPTER 19

Clutch

We'd filled a wagon with wood and beer and dragged the heavy load across the sand. The uneven ground didn't help my knee, and twice, I had to reach down and press my hand against it to staunch the pain. There was still a dull ache in my rib cage, and something told me the injury was going to follow me around for awhile.

A rich, yellow light poured down from the moon, casting long streams of light along the shore. The fire erupted into tall lapping flames within minutes. Taylor had only a thin hooded sweatshirt on, and her smooth, tanned legs were bare.

I sat down in the sand and threw a blanket over my shoulders and held up the corner. Just like the night of the accident, she slid beneath the cover without a word. I lowered my arm and pulled her against me.

Nix and Scotlyn huddled across the pit in their own blanket. Nix threw me a beer but I hardly needed any alcohol. I was drunk already, drunk with the scent of her, the feel of her beneath my fingertips. After she'd crawled into bed with me, all I could think about was having her naked in my arms. I was tired of denying myself the one thing I wanted more than anything.

"Too bad Dray and Cassie couldn't come out tonight,"

Nix said. "Dray's been in a really crappy mood. I think something might be going on with them."

Taylor nestled even closer, and I had to fight back the urge to pull her into my lap. "I haven't talked to him since the party. Maybe Cass is still pissed about the broken patio lights."

"Nah, that's not like Cassie. She hasn't said anything to me at work but then we both keep so busy there, we don't really have time to talk. And I make it a point never to talk about Dray with her. Too many landmines to step on in one of those conversations." Nix looked at Scotlyn. "Have you talked to Cassie lately?"

Scotlyn's profound silence crackled louder than the fire.

"You know something," Nix said.

"It's nothing, and I promised Cassie not to tell anyone. Let's just say it has to do with her photography."

Nix put his arm around her and pulled her against him. "You're not going to tell us?"

Scotyln turned an invisible key in front of her lips.

"Fine. The secret life of women," Nix sighed. "So, what were you two girls up to before we interrupted your little party," Nix asked.

"Oh, nothing much," Scotlyn said. "We were just about to strip and lather each other up in the shower."

My entire body stiffened, but Taylor laughed.

"Holy shit," Nix's voice cracked like the wood in the fire.

Scotlyn shoved him hard, and he fell sideways. "Admit it, you bum, that's the scenario that was going through your imagination when you saw us huddled together on the bow. What do you think we were doing? Girl talk. That's what girls do. And, unlike you guys, sex didn't come up once."

Taylor reached up and poked my cheek with her fingertip. "I think they're both catatonic now."

"Hell yeah, it's going to take me months to get that vision out of my head," Nix said. "What about you, Clutch?"

"Huh? Sorry, I haven't heard anything since she said 'lather'."

Scotlyn laughed. Nix pulled her into his lap and suddenly the fire pit seemed crowded. Taylor seemed to have the same feeling. She pulled off her boots and peered up at me. "Want to take a walk?"

Her mouth was just inches from mine, and I could not stop looking at it. "Yeah, I'd like that."

I stood and then lowered my hand for her to take. As her palm crossed mine, it instantly sent waves of heat up my arm. I wrapped my fingers around her slim hand and pulled her to her feet. We trudged through the cold sand toward the water.

"How's your knee feeling?" she asked. "I wanted to call you this week and see how you were feeling, but my wonderful parents took my phone and computer."

"What is with your parents? They've really gone over the edge lately. And, your brother—" I started, but then decided not to step into the middle. Jason and I had not spoken since the fight, and the strain of it was slowly taking a toll on our partnership. Things had been said that could never be erased. I wondered how often Taylor's parents had told her I wasn't good enough for her. The thought of it had stuck like a knife in my gut all week. My only comfort came from knowing that Taylor had little respect for her parents. In fact, since I'd known her, it always seemed that she'd made a point of doing the exact opposite of their wishes.

"That's all right. You don't have to say anything about Jason. He's my parents' third pair of eyes, and I'm getting tired of it. But I can't understand why he's not getting tired of it."

We'd reached the edge of the beach where the sand dropped down to the water.

Taylor looked down at her bare feet. "Sand is so amazing. It stays boiling hot all day in the sun, and by night fall, it drops to near freezing. I wish I'd kept on my boots. My feet are aching from the cold."

Without hesitation, I leaned down and swept her into my arms. She threw her head back and laughed as her arms circled my neck. "You are feeling better." Then her laughter subsided and she grew quiet. She laid her head down against my shoulder. "You've never carried me in your arms." Her whisper soft tone was nearly lost in the sound of the waves. She didn't lift her face from my chest. "I'm home when I'm in your arms."

I held her tightly and hiked back up toward the deserted bike path. I dropped her incredibly long legs, took hold of her waist and propped her on the small retaining wall that had been built to keep sand off the path. The city had gone through the trouble of putting up light posts along the bike trail, but all of the lights had been broken by vandals. Our bonfire was a good distance away, and the rest of the beach was dark and silent.

Perched on the wall, Taylor's face was almost directly across from mine. A strand of her long hair swept across her mouth, and I reached up and purposely dragged my rough thumb across her bottom lip before pushing the lock of hair behind her ear.

She was uncharacteristically silent as she sat on the wall, looking at me with those unbelievable eyes. "I waver back and forth about a lot of things in my life, but, James Mason, I've never stopped wanting you," she said softly. She reached up and pushed open her sweatshirt revealing the corset style top underneath. The curves of her breasts lifted and fell with each breath.

For the first time, I stood within arm's reach of her without my fists clenched to keep from touching her. I was done battling with myself. I was done reminding myself I couldn't have her.

My fingers pulled the thin ribbon that held together the two sides of her top. The two sides of the fabric fell apart as the ribbon loosened. The rough tips of my calloused fingers slid over her skin as I pushed the sides farther apart. Her perfect breasts, breasts that I'd only seen in my mind until now, stood erect beneath my heated gaze and the cool coastal breeze. Her lush bottom lip dropped as she sucked in a breath. She was still wild and impulsive and she didn't give a damn about what anyone else thought . . . and that was why I was fucking nuts about her.

The slow deliberation with which I moved shocked the hell out of me because more than anything I wanted to drag her off the wall and pull her down beneath me in the sand. My mouth pressed against the soft, creamy skin of her breast, and my tongue drew circles around her nipple.

She tangled her fingers into my hair and pressed her breast harder against my hungry mouth. My hands slid up her bare thighs and without my coaxing she parted her legs slightly. My fingers trailed up the smooth skin of her inner thigh, and her fingers wrapped tighter around my hair as she lifted my face to hers. My mouth came down hard over hers, and she let go of me and grabbed the edge of the wall to keep from falling backward. Reluctantly, I pulled my hands away from the heat between her legs, and my arms wrapped around her. Every movement of her thin body beneath my hands, every tiny sound that escaped her, every inch of her soft skin made me hard with need.

Her head dropped back and my mouth moved down to her throat and neck. A bell rang in the distance, and I pushed it from my mind for a minute but then voices pulled us from the brink of losing all control right there on the beach. Two people were pedaling toward us on bikes.

Taylor's lashes lifted slowly, and she gazed up on me. "Take me home with you, Clutch." She'd whispered the request so softly, it drifted away on the breeze. But every word heated me to the core.

I lifted her off the wall and pulled her behind me through the sand. Nix and Scotlyn had disappeared completely beneath the blanket. Taylor walked around the fire pit and grabbed her boots.

"I'm taking Taylor home," I said.

Nix's thumb came up out of the blanket and then disappeared again.

We half-ran, half-stumbled back to the truck. Taylor held closed her sweatshirt with one hand and held tightly to me with the other. She pressed up against my back as I fumbled to get the keys in the door lock. She slid in across the front seat, and I climbed in behind her. Putting the key into the ignition took just as much effort as opening the door. My mind and body could think of only one thing, and I wasn't completely sure I could get us home safely. I'd been denying myself for so long because I wanted this one girl so badly that no one else would do, and now that my self-control had been completely shattered, I was out of my mind with it.

The engine rumbled and the cab of the truck vibrated. Without warning, Taylor slid her hand across to the buttons on my jeans. She popped open the fly and slid her hand inside my pants.

"I'll never make it home, Taylor."

Her luscious lips turned up in a sly grin. She pulled her hand away, and I nearly fell forward with disappointment. She reached up under her skirt and slid off her panties. "Exactly."

She climbed over to me, straddled my lap, and lowered her mouth to mine. Her sweet breath tickled my chin.

My hands went beneath her skirt and found the bare skin of her perfect ass.

"Do you still have a condom in your wallet?"

I looked up at her. "How did you know about that?"

She kissed me and pressed her smile against my mouth. "I plucked your wallet out of your pocket once. I always made it my job to keep track of everything you were up to."

My fingers caressed her bottom. "Brat. And I guess I have to add pickpocket to my list of Taylor adjectives."

Her tongue swept across my bottom lip. "You have a list

of adjectives?"

"Uh huh," I kissed her mouth and chin and throat. "Bothersome, irritating . . ." My mouth found her breasts again, and she arched her back to push them harder against my mouth. "Irresistible," I whispered against her smooth, hot skin, "fucking amazing." I lifted my face and pulled her mouth toward mine.

Car lights lit up the inside of the cab. "Let's get out of this marina parking lot." I was breathing so hard every word was a struggle.

She kissed me once more and reluctantly climbed off my lap. I backed out of the spot and tore out of the parking lot at drag racing speed. Her hand found my open fly again, and she teased me with her curious fingers.

I groaned and grabbed hold of her wrist. "There's not going to be anything left of me if you keep doing that." I pulled into the first empty parking lot I saw and drove straight to the darkest corner. I reached across to the glove box and pulled out my wallet. And then I looked over at her. Everything about her made me react. Even in the pitch black corner of the parking lot she lit up the interior of the truck like a thousand flickering candles. "I've imagined this moment a billion times but never in the front of this truck. Do you mind?"

She brushed my long hair off my face. "I've imagined this moment a billion times too, and I don't give a shit where it happens. I just want it to happen." She straddled my lap again. Her kisses started gently at first and then increased with intensity.

My hands went beneath her bottom and my fingers slid into her. A silky groan of pleasure rolled from her mouth into mine.

Her fingers pushed back my hair, and she pressed her mouth to my ear. "Make me yours," she whispered.

Chapter 20

Taylor

The ride home seemed slightly surreal. I'd been dreaming of having Clutch all to myself for so long, I found it hard to believe that I was sitting with him, alone in his truck. And even though both his hands had been on the wheel most of the drive home, I could still feel the sensation of his mouth and hands on my skin. We were both silent as we listened to music and got lost in the fact that something had happened between us and that there was no turning back anymore. The usual tension that radiated from him when I was near had changed to hot waves of passion. Now that we'd undone the cork on all of it, it felt as if there would be no way to slow it.

Clutch had driven home at top speed, and he flew into his driveway. Barrett's bike was in front of the garage but the house was dark. I had to suppress a laugh as Clutch struggled again to get the key into his front door lock.

I trailed my fingers down his rock hard back. "Hey, Viking, it's a good thing you have better aim with other things."

He peered at me over his shoulder and shoved the door open. "That's because keys are too small and *other things* aren't." He reached back, grabbed my hand, and pulled me along down the hallway to his room. Once inside the bedroom, he kicked the door shut behind us.

I pushed the sweatshirt off my shoulders, and it puddled on the ground. I reached for the top of his jeans, but he took hold of my hand. Before I knew it, he had both of my wrists caught up in his large fingers. He nearly lifted me off my feet as he dragged me over to the wall and pressed me up against it. He held my wrists above my head and stared down at me hungrily. It sent a rush of heat through me, but my whole body shivered deliciously from the way he looked at me. "I've got to slow you down, my wild, little pickpocket."

His free hand reached up for the ribbon on my top, and with one pull, he had it loosened. His massive chest rose and fell sharply with each breath as his fingers parted the corset top to expose my naked breasts. His eyes didn't leave my breasts as he reached behind the small of my back and unfastened my skirt. It slipped to the floor and he pushed my panties down next. The cool air in the room circulated around my naked legs. I struggled to free my wrists, but he held them tightly. He leaned down and trailed his tongue around my ear and neck and his free hand smoothed down my abdomen to the moist heat between my legs.

The vulnerability of being trapped in his hand only increased my need for him, and instinctively, I moved my hips against the movement of his hand. I cried out as his movements increased in pressure and speed. He covered my mouth with his, and I could barely catch my breath as his fingers moved inside me. The luxurious strokes of his rough finger tips pushed me to the edge, and the heat, the movement, the pressure on my skin exploded into waves of ecstasy. He held tightly to my wrists to keep me from sinking to the ground in a heap. Then he pulled me into his arms.

My hands finally free, I took hold of the hem of his shirt and slid it up above the hard ridges of his chest muscles. My tongue traced along every line of his taut stomach and it danced back and forth over the dark line of hair that bisected his abdomen. He whipped the shirt off over his head and dropped it to the floor. I'd seen him shirtless before, and it always took my breath away.

Before I could reach for the fly of his jeans, he had me in his arms. He carried to me to the bed and laid me down. His heavy gaze drifted over my naked body leaving wicked trails of heat on my skin.

"Christ, Taylor, you are unreal." He unbuttoned his pants and pushed them to the floor. I held my breath as he reached down and pushed apart my legs. He knelt between them and then winced in pain. "Damn, I forgot about my knee." He smiled and rolled onto his back bringing me along with him. I placed my hands on his chest and sat up, my thighs straddling him. It had only been a few minutes, but the surge of moist heat between my legs assured me that I wanted him again . . . badly.

His arm reached back, and he fished blindly in his dresser drawer for a condom. He pulled out a deck of cards. I laughed.

"Is that for when you invite a girl over for romantic night of Gin Rummy?"

"Strip poker." He dropped the cards on the floor and kept searching. He pulled out a pair of black sunglasses with one of the lenses missing.

I laughed again. "And you are keeping those because—?"

"They're from my past life as a one-eyed pirate. Ah ha," he said victoriously and held up a condom.

I plucked it from his hand and instantly the light conversation stopped, and his lids got heavy as he gazed up at me. His massive chest moved up and down with each quick breath as I wrapped my fingers around him. He was solid and smooth and incredible as I rolled the condom down the hard, hot length of him.

His thick, calloused fingers reached down and grabbed my arms, pulling me back up toward him. My face lowered over his and my mouth came down roughly on his. A deep groan rolled up from his throat as my tongue swept across his. His fingers pressed into the flesh of my hips as the kiss deepened. The urge to have him inside of me was overwhelming. I lifted my mouth from his and watched his face as I slid over him. His pelvis moved to meet me and his grasp on me tightened. I reached up and wrapped my fingers around the rod iron bed board. His hands moved to my bottom, and he held me firmly as we rocked hard against each other building in speed and intensity.

I closed my eyes feeling every inch of him inside of me. My thighs tightened as I rocked back and forth wanting him to move even deeper. Every thrust, every movement touched my core. His grip tightened again and I moved against him. My head spun from the intensity of it, and I lost my grip on the headboard and collapsed to his chest. My mind was swept into the warm darkness, and the only physical feeling remaining was that of Clutch moving inside of me. I clamped down tightly on him, wanting him to stay there forever as I went over the edge.

His fingers bit almost painfully into the flesh of my hips as he pulled me against him. I pressed my face against his shoulder and muffled a scream as deep spasms of sheer ecstasy pulsed through me. His movements quickened, and I ached with pleasure. Then his grasp tightened, and his back arched off the mattress. A deep moan rolled from his lips and he relaxed. His arms went around me as I pressed my face against his chest.

I sighed contentedly wondering if this was all really happening. "I have to say, my imagination was pretty spot on. That was just how I thought it would be."

His fingers skimmed over my back sending a shiver through me. "You've been imagining it?"

I lifted my face and stared down at him. "Haven't you?"

He reached down and pulled the cover up over us. "Don't know if I should answer that on grounds that it might incriminate me."

I lowered my head to his chest again, and his arm tightened around me. "You do realize that this was all meant to be."

He kissed the top of my head. "Yep, I've known it all along."

Strange waves of light drifted in through his bedroom window, and for a moment, I thought I was still high from the drugging effect his touch had had on me. But then a loud explosion of glass breaking startled both of us. Clutch released me and I rolled off of him.

Barrett's feet pounded down the hallway, and he pushed open the bedroom door. He was pulling on his jeans and his phone was pressed to his ear as he glanced into the room. He did a double take when he saw me. "Aimee's house is on fire," he blurted, and then disappeared down the hallway.

Clutch flew out of bed and pulled on his clothes. I got

dressed and ran out behind him. Black smoke filled the front yard as flames shot straight up through the roof of the neighbor's house. Clutch and Barrett were leaning over someone who was sitting on the grass.

I reached them just as Barrett gave the dazed looking guy a rough shake. "Where's Aimee?" he yelled. Billows of smoke seeped from every corner of the house. The whole place was ablaze, and the heat and acrid smell swirled around us like an inferno. Other sleepy, confused neighbors began stumbling from their homes, gasping in shock and horror.

The guy glanced back at the house. "I think she's still in the bedroom."

Barrett released his hold on the guy and raced to the back gate. Clutch went to follow but the guy grabbed his leg. "It's too late. The whole place is in flames. You can't save her."

Clutch shook off the guy's hold on his leg. Through the haze of smoke I could see Clutch scowl down at the guy and then his arm drew back and he punched him in the face. The neighbor landed flat on his back and yelled in pain.

"You've had that coming for a long time, you asshole," Clutch sneered and then raced to the backyard.

I ran behind him and reached them just as Barrett heaved a large planter through the glass pane. Smoke poured out into the cool night air. "Aimee!" he yelled into the opening. Without hesitation, he dove through the window that was bordered with jagged glass.

Clutch climbed in behind him, and the true terror of it all suddenly struck me. I'd never been so close to a burning house, and it was beyond frightening. It seemed the fire would devour everything in its path. The smoke made visibility and breathing impossible. I pulled my sweatshirt up over my nose and mouth, but my eyes burned with stinging pain. In the distance, I heard the sirens, but it all seemed too little, too late. I cut my fingers as I grasped the edge of the shattered window. I couldn't see anything inside, but I heard some movement and coughing.

"Over hear, Clutch, Barrett. The window is over here." I sucked in a breath and nearly choked on it. Tears flooded my eyes both from smoke and the sheer horror of thinking something had happened to them. "Over here," I cried. The sirens grew louder and then stopped. The red flashing lights out front gave the black plumes of smoke an eerie quality, and a cold chill grabbed hold of my heart. I took a deep breath and pressed my face farther into the room. The smoke was like a thick, wool cloak, completely opaque and suffocating. The chemicals from the wood, paint and other materials in the burning house smelled toxic and a wave of nausea seized me. "Clutch, damn it, where are you?" There was no echo back. The tone of my voice was absorbed by the poisonous, viscous haze. "Clutch!" I screamed with the small bit of oxygen I had left in my lungs.

Then a giant blond head loomed in the window, and a cry of joy spilled from my lips. "Grab her arms, Taylor." The girl was small and pale and flopped over the rough edge of the window like a rag doll. I lifted her up to avoid the shards of glass and pulled her out. I fell back on the grass and held her head in my lap. Tears of relief flowed from my eyes as both Clutch and Barrett jumped out of the window. Barrett collapsed to his knees, coughing and shuddering in pain.

Clutch's face and shirt were covered with soot. He

braced his hands on his thighs as he leaned down to catch his breath.

I rubbed my fingers over the girl's face and smeared away some of the ashes. She didn't respond to my touch at first but then her shoulders twitched and she coughed. Smoke still billowed from the window as a spray of water arced up high in the air and covered the flames on the roof. I looked up at Clutch. "You need to get her out to fresher air."

He swept the girl up in his arms and carried her toward the front yard. She coughed several more times, which was comforting to hear. Two firemen met Clutch at the back gate. "My brother's hurt too," he told them as he handed the girl off to a fireman.

I stumbled over to Barrett. His naked chest was covered with blood from the glass.

Barrett's face was pale and sweaty. He leaned forward and my hand flew to my mouth to stifle a gasp. His naked back was blistered with burns. I dropped to my knees and pressed my hand against his face. "Hold on, Sweetie, help is here." I removed my sweatshirt and wiped the rivulets of blood that streamed down his chest. His whole body trembled as he leaned against me for support.

Clutch raced through the back gate with two paramedics. "Let's see if we can move him away from the house," one of the paramedics suggested.

Clutch took hold of Barrett's hand and pulled his arm over his shoulder. Barrett's bare feet lifted off the ground as Clutch stood to full height and carried him across the yard and away from the choking clouds of smoke.

Barrett's face was so twisted in pain, I felt his agony in

my chest and stomach. He held tightly to my hand as they administered first aid to his cuts and took his vitals.

Clutch's face was white with worry. "Rett, hang in there, Buddy. It doesn't look as bad as I thought." The waver in his tone brought tears to my eyes. Clutch was always sturdy, cocky and in complete control, but this had shattered his normally unflappable confidence.

The paramedic took down Barrett's name and age and called his vitals in to the hospital. The second paramedic turned to Clutch. "Do you all live here?"

"No, the guy on the front lawn and the girl they just carried out live here. We're neighbors."

"And you both climbed through that window to reach her?"

Clutch nodded.

"I guess you two are definitely the heroes of the night. His back looks worse than it is. It's blistering up fast though, and we definitely need to get him to the hospital." The paramedic looked back toward the house where tufts of smoke slithered over the broken window edge and then coiled into rings before disappearing into the night air. "You're both lucky you made it back out. People jump into burning buildings not realizing that the smoke is blinding."

Clutch nodded. "Couldn't see anything and we lost our bearings once we climbed inside." Clutch looked over at me, and his blue eyes held more emotion than I'd ever seen in them. "Then a sweet angel called us to the window." His throat moved up and down as he swallowed. "Thank you," he said quietly to me. "If you hadn't been there—"

"Told you it was meant to be," I said softly back to him.

A voice floated over our heads. "Jimmy." We looked up. An older man who I'd seen walk out onto his front porch moments earlier stood behind us. He looked at Barrett and Clutch. "You two boys are really something else. Aimee is sitting up with an oxygen mask."

"Thank God," Clutch said.

The elderly man looked down at the ground and then back up at Clutch. "That's why I hate to tell you this, Jimmy. While you two were saving Aimee, the fire jumped over to your garage. It's gone."

Clutch looked as if someone had just struck him the chest with a cannon ball.

Barrett muttered through his pain. "Go, Jimmy, I'll be fine."

I followed Clutch out to the front yard. The entire block was standing in the street watching the drama unfold. Two fire trucks and two ambulances lined the curb. There were at least four police cars too.

The flames were extinguished and only bitter remnants of moist smoke hovered over the scene. Clutch's truck and Barrett's bike stood in front of wisps of smoke and ash, but the garage was gone. Inside the framing that remained, the burnt out of shell of a car leered back at us from its smoky grave.

"Was that the Shelby Jason told me about?" I asked.

Clutch's face dropped and the sadness in his expression brought tears back to my eyes. I took hold of his hand, and he wrapped his fingers in mine.

"At least everyone is still alive," I said weakly.

He kissed the top of my head, and we walked over to

where Aimee sat on the raised gurney. Aimee's husband was standing on the sidewalk talking to several policemen. He held an ice pack against his face.

Aimee lifted the oxygen mask from her face when she saw Clutch. "James," her voice was shaky and hoarse, "you and Barrett saved my life. I'm so sorry about your garage."

Clutch stepped up to the gurney and took hold of her hand. "I'm just glad you're all right."

The two policemen walked over to us. Aimee's husband followed behind almost as if he was hiding behind the two officers. He seemed nervous to get near Clutch and with good reason. Clutch had really nailed him.

"James Mason?" one of the officers said.

"Yeah, that's me."

"You're under arrest for assault. Your neighbor claims you attacked him as his house burned down."

Clutch looked past the officers to his neighbor. "You fucking weasel."

Aimee took off her mask. "Officers, this man saved my life. You can't possibly be thinking of arresting him. I would have died." She pointed at her husband, who still cowered behind the policemen. "I'm sure my husband fell asleep on the couch with his cigarette. He's done it before. And while he managed to get himself safely out of the house, he never even tried to save me." She put her hand to her mouth and coughed.

Clutch put a bracing hand on her shoulder until she could catch her breath again. "It's all right, Aimee, save your breath."

She shook her head and swallowed. "Mr. Mason and

his brother risked their lives and dove into a house that was completely engulfed in flames. I'm certain I was just moments from succumbing to the smoke when they found me." She looked over at her husband. "We are officially through, you bastard." Her voice shook. "And if you don't drop the charges, Dustin, then I will let everyone know what a coward you were tonight. All of your friends, your brothers, your parents, everyone will know that you climbed out of a burning house and left me behind."

Everyone, including the officers, turned to look at the jerk. The side of his face was swollen and red from the ice pack. The guy looked as if he wanted to melt into the sidewalk below his feet. He walked away without another word.

One of the police officers turned back to Clutch and put out his hand. "Well done, Sir."

Barrett was wheeled out on a gurney, and the entire neighbor burst into applause and cheers. Tears streamed down my face as I took hold of Clutch's arm. "He'll be O.K. right?"

"No one snaps back from bad stuff faster than Rett." He pulled his arm from my grasp and dropped it around my shoulder. Then he squeezed me against his hard body. "Definitely a night I will never forget. For a lot of reasons."

CHAPTER 21

Taylor

It was well past midnight by the time we left the hospital. Barrett had received second degree burns across his shoulders, and he needed fifteen stitches in the cuts on his chest. The doctors admitted him for a few days. I'd sent my mom a simple text that told her I was fine and hanging out with friends. She was pissed enough not to answer. Even though I was through lying about my whereabouts, I was also not in the mood to let her know where I was. Sometimes withholding information was the easiest route.

I sat next to Clutch and rested my head on his hard shoulder as we drove home. The rough ride of the truck nearly lulled me to sleep. Clutch looked as tired as I felt. In the course of one short evening, we'd experienced every high caliber emotion in the human spectrum, and I felt the fatigue of it deep in my bones. And in the chaos of the night, our relationship had changed so significantly, I was still not certain where we'd landed.

"Do you think the burns will leave him with a lot of scars on his back?" I asked.

"The doctor thought that he'd heal up pretty well." He laughed weakly. "Besides, the way Rett likes to strut around without his shirt on, he'll probably welcome a few battle scars."

"True. I guess he probably doesn't have any health insurance, does he?"

He laughed again and it sounded weary. "Barrett can't afford to buy himself a box of bandages, let alone insurance." He sighed. "I'll call my parents tomorrow and let them know what happened, but I'm sure I'll have to pay his bills. I'm more worried about the fight I'm going to have with the insurance company over that car. Your brother is going to spit fire when I tell him. He's already pissed at me."

I wrapped my arms around his massive arm and hugged it tightly. "Jason is always pissed these days. I think he's unhappy with his personal life, and he's taking it out on everyone else. You may have noticed that his girlfriend is a charmless, stick-up-the-ass bitch."

A smile dented his cheek. "I might have noticed." The smile disappeared as quickly as it had appeared. "Jason told me your parents don't want me anywhere near you."

"Fuck them."

"Yeah," he said with little conviction.

I pressed my face against his arm. "Can I stay with you tonight?"

He paused and a nervous flutter went through my stomach. "I was hoping you would."

The ugly, scorched remnants of the bizarre night met us at the top of his driveway. His house stood lonely and sad on the otherwise empty lot. We climbed out of the car and walked inside. Clutch turned on some music and plopped down hard on the couch.

"I can still taste the smoke. I need some water," I said.

"Do you want a glass?"

He nodded almost imperceptibly. I walked into the kitchen and filled two glasses with water and returned to the living room. The music vibrated off the walls. Clutch's ridiculously long legs stretched out across the floor, and he stared at the wall. I'd seen him excited, angry, in pain and everything in between, but this was the heart-wrenching look of defeat on his face, a face I knew better than my own. I drank the water and swallowed back the pain brought on by seeing him look so incredibly sad.

I handed him some water. He finished it quickly, and I placed the glasses on the coffee table. I sat on my knees facing him. His profile looked as if an artist had chiseled it out of stone.   "Jason will get over the car. And my parents could never say anything that would change my opinion of you."

His face dropped and he looked down at his hands. His knuckles were red and raw from the fire. I took hold of his hand, lifted it to my mouth, and pressed my lips against his burned skin. I lowered his hand to his lap and pushed long strands of blond hair back behind his ear. My lips caressed his temple and then his ear and then his stubble covered chin. He sat perfectly still as I kissed his neck and his shoulder. I crawled around and straddled his lap. I took hold of his face and lifted it. It was a face that had invaded most of my daydreams. It was a face that always took my breath away, no matter what mood he was in, even now in the terrible darkness that seemed to have taken hold of him. His long, dark lashes fluttered down as I kissed his eyebrow and nose.

I kissed his mouth lightly. His eyes were still closed.

"There has never been anyone but you, Clutch. I still remember the day when I realized that I wanted you and no one else." His blue eyes lifted and I smiled as I kissed his chin. "You and Jason had picked me up from school. A lady's car was stuck in the middle of the road. She looked terrified as the traffic swooshed past her." I picked up his hand and kissed his palm. "You'd been telling Jason about rebuilding some motor, and you pulled over and held up your giant hand to stop the cars. You walked over, helped the lady into her car and pushed the stalled car to the side of the road. Then you got back in your car and started up the conversation about the motor. What you'd done was no big deal to you, but no one else had taken the time to help her. I remember watching you from the back seat with those same big hands gripping the steering wheel, and all I could think was someday I want those massive arms to hold me. I knew nothing bad could happen to me wrapped in those unbelievable arms." I kissed him again and his arms circled me. He held me with a crushing force that nearly swept the breath from me, and yet, I wanted him to hold me tighter.

CHAPTER 22

Taylor

Jasmine came up next to me as I crossed the lawn to the sidewalk. "You're always hoofing it these days. What happened? Did your mom's car break down?"

"Nope. She doesn't ever let me use it anymore. She seems to think I can get into even more trouble with a car. Fortunately, I don't mind walking, but I want to find a job and I'm kind of limited without transportation." After I'd spent the entire night with Clutch, my mom had stopped talking to me completely. But I was in such a state of bliss about being with him, I couldn't have cared less. In fact, it was less stressful not talking to her. She had no idea who I was seeing, and I didn't need to cause Clutch anymore grief by telling her. I'd decided it was none of her damn business, or my dad's, or Jason's, for that matter.

Jasmine took hold of my arm and pulled me toward the parking lot. "Well, I've got a car today. Let's go hang out at the taco stand. We never get to talk anymore."

"I don't know, Jaz, Adam and his buddies will be there. And if he's there, then I'm sure his new girlfriend, Chelsea, will be there. She really hates me. They all do."

Jasmine stopped and put her hands on her hips. "Taylor Flinn, since when do you give a shit what those dorks think?" She looked pleadingly at me. "I want to hear about that guy from Alaska. Kiley said you were seeing him on the sly. Come on, please."

"Fine, for a little while, but you're going to be disappointed because we are just friends. He might have even gone back up north again."

We trudged along to the parking lot. "Well, you're up to something. I can see it in the way you walk."

I laughed. "Jeez, you sound like my mom." I held back a smile thinking about what I had been up to, but I had no intention of telling Jasmine about Clutch. She'd teased me about my crush on him mercilessly for the past two years, and while it seemed natural that I would want to gloat about it to her, I really didn't care if she knew. And everything was so new that I still felt on shaky ground when it came to Clutch. Now that I'd left myself wide open and vulnerable, it seemed one strong breeze could push me over to heartbreak. I'd wanted Clutch for so long it was all still just too unreal for me to believe.

As usual, half the student body was parked at the taco stand. Adam's tall head stood up across the way, and Chelsea's blonde hair sparkled beneath her blue head band. I followed behind Jasmine reluctantly, and while most people had grown bored of the Taylor and Adam saga, Adam's crew of snobby friends had not. They all turned to look at me as we crossed the lot to the order window.

Jasmine rolled her eyes. "Here we are at the last quarter of high school, and they still act like they're in elementary school. Just ignore them."

"I usually do." My phone buzzed and I slid it out of the pocket of my shorts. It was just a text but even his short messages made my heart fly ahead of its usual pace.

"I'm going to the hospital to visit Rett. Want to go?"

"Yes," I wrote back immediately.

"Where are you at?"

"I'm at the taco stand."

"Perfect. I'm hungry and Barrett was whining about the hospital food. Be there in fifteen."

"Who was that?" Jasmine asked. "Whoever it was, it sure turned your frown upside down fast." She grabbed my arm. "Was it the fisherman?"

"No. I told you I'm not seeing him."

She looked disappointed.

"Sorry not to be able to provide you with tawdry details of my dating life. What about you, Jaz? What happened to that older guy from work?"

She waved off the question. "Turns out he was only interested in one thing." Her attention had turned back to the parking lot, and she seemed to be searching for someone. Just then a motorcycle pulled into the lot and she nearly danced with excitement.

"Who's that?" I asked.

"That is my new honey. He's my neighbor's cousin."

"See and you wanted to hear about my life while you had all sorts of goodies stored up to tell me."

She leaned toward me. "He's so fucking hot, and he's all man. My mom is pissed as hell of course, but I don't care. I'm crazy about him."

He stretched up tall in his leathers as he stepped off his bike, but as he took off his helmet the layers of hotness disappeared. His head was shaved clean and he had tattoos across his bare scalp. He made Gus look like the boy next door.

Jasmine held her breath as he walked toward us.

"Gee, I can't imagine why your mom would be pissed."

Our school mates stared with wide open mouths as he approached us. Jasmine turned to me. "I hope you don't mind that I invited him."

"Actually, it works out fine. I've got a friend picking me up in a few minutes. I'm just going to get a drink and wait for him."

Jasmine turned to me. "Him?"

"Uh huh."

Her new friend had reached us. "Rick, this is my friend, Taylor."

"Hey, Rick. Well, I'm heading to the order window. It was nice meeting you." I was relieved to have a reason to leave, and since Jasmine was now occupied, I couldn't get out of there fast enough.

Adam and his judgmental crew were sitting along the tables near the order window. I ignored their glares and got into line. I heard Chelsea's distinctive snicker. I'd heard it before in the hallway at school and it had reminded me of a hyena.

"Rumor has it, no one has asked her to the prom. Skanks don't usually attend, you know." Chelsea sneered in my direction but once again I ignored her.

"Is that true, Flinn?" One of Adam's football friends asked. "I'd take you. I'll bet you're a whole lot of fun up in the hotel room after the prom."

"Nah, she's not that much fun. She's pretty selfish when it comes to sex." Adam chimed in next, and his words felt like nails in my back. Laughter roared around his table.

The line was moving at a snail's pace, and I considered just ditching the drink idea. But if I left, they would know they'd gotten to me. So I stood my ground and reminded myself that they were idiots. Adam was the biggest douche of all. Obviously, the break up had shattered his ego a lot more than he'd let on.

"Hey," Clutch texted, "I'm almost there. Get in line. Four fish tacos and two chicken."

"I'm in line but hurry."

A text came right back. "What's wrong?"

"Nothing. Just hurry and get me out of here."

I'd moved up several spaces but not out of earshot of the barrage of insults being fired at me from Adam's table. Chelsea seemed to be taking extra pleasure in attacking me. I had no idea why since she'd already landed Adam, and I had nothing more to do with him.

"Her parents should send her back to the east coast. Maybe she could still get a prom date over there."

They were quite focused on prom, a senior event that had never even crossed my mind. From what I'd heard, they'd even decided on a corny disco theme. I couldn't imagine anything more boring.

For a moment, they fell silent and I was relieved. There was just one person in front of me.

I ordered and scooted over to the pick-up line, which was even closer to the table of clowns, but they seemed to have run out of ammo. I made a point of staring at the pick-up window to avoid any eye contact with them, but then something hit my back and they erupted in laughter again.

"Ah, come on," Adam's friend said, "I thought a quarter would at least get me a blow job."

His comment had now gotten the attention of other people in line and everyone turned to stare at me. I'd always had a reputation for being wild, but I'd never done anything to be deemed a slut. My eyes ached as I blinked back tears.

I recognized Adam's laugh behind me. "Hey, Taylor, here comes that big dude you have a crush on. Maybe you should ask him to the prom." Everyone laughed. "I'm sure he'd jump at the chance."

I looked back across the lot. The crowd milling in front of the taco stand parted and everyone stared as Clutch walked through. He was always an amazing and imposing sight to see, and it seemed even the tables and umbrellas scooted over to let him through. But he didn't notice the people gawking and staring. His gaze found me, and instantly, I felt like I was standing alone. Suddenly, all the harsh, ugly words meant nothing at all. Everything about the man stole my breath away. My heart raced as he neared, and Adam's table fell noticeably silent behind me.

Clutch smiled down at me but then seemed to sense my distress. "Everything all right?"

I glanced at Adam's table. He looked as if he'd just been stung in the ass by a wasp. "It is now," I said quietly.

They called our number and Clutch grabbed the bag of food. We headed back to the truck. Most of the conversations stopped abruptly as we walked back through. I caught a glimpse of Jasmine and her new friend. She looked even more shocked than Adam. Clutch still took no notice of the disruption he'd caused with his arrival.

I was relieved to reach his truck. He placed the food on the hood and went to unlock my door but then stopped. He turned around and took hold of my face and lifted it up toward his mouth. Then he leaned down and kissed me. "I confess, I've been thinking about nothing else but those plump lips of yours all day."

I reached up and slid my arms around his neck and kissed him back. "And I've been thinking about nothing but those arms around me all day."

He smiled down at me. "Then I guess neither of us got much accomplished." His eyes drifted down to the neckline of my blouse and then his dark lashes lifted. "I think we should stop by my house on the way to the hospital. I've got some *things* to tend to before we go see Barrett." Discretely, his hand reached up between us and he slid his thumb over the fabric stretched across my breast. I sucked in a breath.

I licked my lip. "Sounds important. We should definitely stop home."

We climbed into the truck, and I tucked myself tightly against him. I glanced out the window toward the taco stand. Adam's harsh glare shot daggers at me across the parking lot. I'd just endured some of the meanest words anyone had ever spit at me, and while they'd come from people I'd grown up with, people I'd spent years going to school with, none of it mattered. The only person that mattered to me was the person sitting next to me. He was the only person who could truly hurt me. For a second I closed my eyes and then opened them again. He was still there, all six foot plus of him with his long blond hair, strong chin, and the confidence of a man in charge of the world. I took hold of his rock hard arm and wondered if he realized just how easily he could crush my heart.

CHAPTER 23

Clutch

Once again I found myself driving like a man on fire through the crowded streets of Los Angeles, clutching the steering wheel so hard it nearly crumbled in my hands. I had no shred of control left when it came to Taylor. The tacos that had sounded so good on the way to the taco stand had lost all their appeal once I'd tasted Taylor's lips again. Now my hunger had an entirely different focus. I knew once I'd allowed myself the pleasure of touching her that I would not be able to stop wanting her and I'd been right.

My tires chirped as they hit the driveway at a ridiculous speed. I turned off the car, and we hurried inside. The house was hot and stuffy, but opening windows would have taken too much time and effort.

I grabbed Taylor and held her arms tightly as I kissed her hard and deep. Her fingers clutched the fabric of my shirt as if she needed to hold onto something to keep her balance. This time I was the one that needed to slow down, but it seemed impossible.

My hands moved to the buttons on her blouse. Her hands reached to the bottom of my shirt and we parted mouths just long enough for me to slide my t-shirt off over my head. She pulled her lips from mine and looked up at me, and I swallowed a sharp breath.

My hand reached up and I pressed my palm against her cheek. "If you only knew how hard it has been for me to deny myself these past few years. It's been torture."

"I think I have some idea." She took hold of my wrist and placed my palm over her heart. It stuttered wildly beneath my touch. Then she leaned closer and pressed her mouth against the bare skin of my chest. Her tongue and lips trailed down my abdomen to the top of my jeans. Her fingers deftly opened up my fly and she pushed my pants to the floor. A groan caught in my throat as she took hold of me and traced the hard tip with her tongue. She straightened and stepped away from me. She licked her bottom lips and stared at me. "You take my breath away, James Mason."

Then she slid the open blouse off her smooth brown shoulders and slid her shorts and panties to the ground. She was flawless, and as many times as I'd imagined her naked, nothing had compared to the real thing.

She reached back and pulled the ribbon she had tied in her hair. Her copper hair cascaded around her shoulders. A sly, sultry smile tipped up her plump lips as she held the ribbon up to me. "Come on, Viking, you'll never need to deny yourself again."

My heart slammed back and forth against my ribs as I took the ribbon from her hand. Taylor was wild and passionate in every aspect of life, just as I'd expected. Even though she was completely naked and just handed me her ribbon with a pleading, hungry look in her eyes, she sat demurely, almost shyly, on the bed.

I stared down at her, and every fantasy I'd ever had about having Taylor naked beneath me raced through my head. I motioned for her to lie back on the bed. Her perfect, full breasts rose and fell as her breaths came quicker and shorter. I could not stop looking at her, stretched-out, supple and aching for me to touch her. I balled the ribbon up in my fist.

"Turn on your stomach." The words cracked out of my throat.

She hesitated but only for a second. I leaned down and lightly bit her round bottom. She half giggled-half squealed in pleasure. I straddled her legs, not allowing the full force of my weight to rest on her. I ran my mouth along her side and then across her shoulders. Her thin body shivered beneath me. I reached up and tied one end of the ribbon loosely around her wrist. I pulled it through the rod iron railing of my bed and then I tied her other wrist.

She mewled softly as I ran a long line of kisses down the center of her back until I reached her bottom. My hand slid beneath her and my fingers found the moist heat between her legs. She sucked in a breath as my fingers massaged the warm folds. Her bottom lifted toward my mouth and my tongue trailed over her bare skin. I pushed her bottom higher exposing every inch of her to my mouth.

"Clutch," her voice shot out on a breathless whisper.

She pressed her face into the pillow to muffle a cry as she met my hungry mouth with her heated flesh. I tasted every sweet bit of her as her body moved rhythmically with every stroke of my tongue. My fingers continued to smooth over the hot nub as my mouth and tongue explored her intimately. Her bound hands gripped the bars of the head board, and she no longer muffled her screams. My hand and mouth moved faster and deeper until I felt the heat of her cascade around my tongue. Her cries of ecstasy filled the air and made me so hard I thought I would lose control. I leaned over and grabbed the condom from the night stand.

I reached up and pulled free the ribbon and she twisted onto her back. She reached down and took hold of me. Using one hand to brace myself, I slid my free hand beneath her bottom and lifted her toward me. I pushed inside of her. She moaned with pleasure as I pulled her harder against me.

Her fingernails dug into my arms as she threw her long legs around my back and took me in deeper and deeper with each thrust. She screamed out again, and I could not hold back. I pushed into her and waves of release pulsed through my taut muscles.

I fell in a breathless, mindless heap next to her on the bed, and I pulled her into my arms.

***

The nurse behind the desk looked up at me and her eyes widened. "Oh my, you must be Mr. Mason's brother. Amazing family resemblance." She stood and looked up at me. "And I thought he was big. How on earth did your parents keep the refrigerator stocked? I'll show you to his room. I've been meaning to head down there." She scuttled around from her desk and Taylor and I followed her fast stride. The nurse looked back over her shoulder at us. "I sent three volunteers up to geriatrics forty minutes ago, but they have mysteriously vanished. I believe it has something to do with your brother." We reached a room with a door ajar and female giggles drifted out to the hallway. The nurse sighed loudly and stepped inside.

Barrett was sitting up in bed, shirtless, of course, which may or may not have had to do with his injury. It was hard to know with my brother. Three girls in striped uniform dresses hovered over his bed. The terrified look they gave the nurse assured us that they were the missing volunteers.

The nurse cleared her throat loudly. "Girls, this is definitely not geriatrics. Now get up there or I won't sign off on your hours."

One of the girls made a point of touching Barrett's shoulder before bidding him farewell.

The nurse walked over and checked the I.V. bag. "Mr. Mason, your arrival has disrupted the volunteer program considerably. I suppose it's a good thing you're leaving us tomorrow. Then we can get back to normal around here."

Barrett smiled up at her as she leaned over him and checked the tubes in his hand. "You know you're going to miss me when I'm gone."

"Just like I'd miss a bunion on my foot." The nurse looked back at me. "Is he always like this?"

"You mean annoying? Yes, yes he is."

Taylor laughed. The nurse left the room.

Barrett pointed at my hand. "I thought you were bringing tacos."

"We had the tacos," I glanced over at Taylor, "but we got sidetracked."

Barrett lifted his brow. "I'll bet you did. Here I am, suffering in the hospital with burns and you two are whooping it up. I guess it's a good thing one of the volunteers brought me a burger and fries."

Taylor sat on the edge of his bed. "Cute girls in little

striped dresses fawning over you and bringing you burgers, your suffering has been great indeed."

"Yeah," Barrett said with dramatic flourish. "Still, I'll be glad to get the hell out of here tomorrow. Hey, Jimmy, did you meet Aimee's parents? They've been here all day. Nice people. Rich."

"Her parents? But I thought they wanted nothing to do with her?"

"When they heard that she'd almost died, they came right away." Barrett reached over to his dresser for a candy bar that had been left there. He held it up. "Sweetest little night nurse brought me this from the cafeteria."

"You're friggin' ridiculous," I said. "So, what about her parents? They've made up?"

"Looks that way. I guess all it takes is almost losing someone to make your realize how much you love them." Barrett stared down at the chocolate in his hand, and his face darkened some. "I know you called Mom and Dad. They never came to see me."

Taylor flashed me a quick look and then she reached over and helped him fold down the foil on the candy. "Your parents hate driving on the freeway, don't they? Otherwise, I'm sure they would've come."

"Yeah, I guess." He laid the candy back on the table and leaned back slowly. He winced as his bandaged shoulders rested against the pillow. The topic of our parents had taken the wind out of him. Being the youngest, he still held onto that slim bit of hope that my parents would suddenly become involved and interested in our lives, but that would never happen. It wasn't in their nature. And just like Taylor's parents were overbearing and too concerned about her life, our parents were way too removed from ours.

Unfamiliar voices sounded in the hallway and a couple walked into Barrett's room. It was easy to see that they were Aimee's parents. Her mom had the same sweet smile and spray of freckles. Barrett had been right. They smelled of money.

Aimee's father stuck out his hand. "You must be Barrett's brother, James. Aimee speaks highly of you. I'm David Peters and this is my wife, Bianca. We can't thank you enough for what your brother and you did, risking your lives to save our Aimee."

"I'm just glad we were there to pull her out safely. This is Taylor. She was there that night as well. It was her voice that guided us out of the smoke."

Mr. Peters walked over and stuck out his hand again. "Thank you, Taylor."

"You're entirely welcome."

Aimee's father reached into his pocket and pulled out his wallet and looked back at me. "I understand that you lost a sixty-five Shelby in the fire." He shook his head. "Terrible tragedy. I'm a bit of a classic car collector myself, and I have many friends with heavy pockets and a weakness for vintage cars." He handed me a business card. "Please send me the information for your parts business. I think I can send a flood of clients your way, and I'll keep my ears open about a replacement for that Shelby. Oh, and I insist on paying your brother's hospital bills."

"Thank you, Sir, but that's not necessary."

He held up his hand. "No, I insist. I've already made arrangements for the bill to be sent to me. It's the least I can do."

I didn't know how to respond. It had been the most generous thing anyone had ever done for me. "Your daughter, Aimee, is an incredible person. She works hard and deserves happiness. I'm glad you have found each other again."

Mr. Peters looked back at his wife and then back at me. "Sometimes, as parents, we make stupid decisions, and we have certainly learned our lesson. Our pride got in the way, but that's all changed."

I glanced over at Taylor. Her gaze had dropped and she stared down at the floor, but I knew exactly what she was thinking.

"Well, we're going back over to Aimee's room. Stop by and say hello to her when you get a chance," Mr. Peters said.

"I will."

They left.

"You know," Barrett said with a yawn, "I've been thinking— maybe I'll become a firefighter. I kind of like that whole facing danger aspect of it all."

Taylor shook her head. "That's just what you need— a fireman's uniform. You've already got the whole female world turned upside down. I can only imagine."

Barrett blinked with feigned astonishment. "What do you mean? Do girls like firemen?"

She went to smack him on the arm but then thought better of it. "Even injured, you are still such an ass."

"But I'm serious. I think I'd be good at it."

I pulled up a chair and sat. "I guess you think you can just snap your fingers and you'll land yourself a job with a fire squad. Doesn't happen like that, Rett. Those jobs are hard to get, and they require a lot of training."

Once again, he looked deflated. "What the hell am I going to do, Jimmy? I can't clean oil off of car parts all my life."

I looked around at the barren hospital room with its pale mint green walls. "Apparently, you've been having a lot of time to reflect while you've been sitting here. Just get healed up and then you can start thinking about it, Rett." My conversation with my dad had gone as I'd expected. His reaction to Barrett's jumping into a burning house to save a life and his subsequent injuries had been met with the same emotional reaction as if I'd told him the weather. He had shown some emotion though— anger about Barrett getting kicked off of the boat. That's when I realized that Barrett could never go back home. It wasn't the kind of home you went back to. My parents were like sea turtles, once you left the nest, you were on your own to fight for survival. And we'd all left the nest for good. "Rett, you know you can stay with me for as long as you need."

He nodded. "Thanks, Bro, you've always been there for me."

"So, they're releasing you tomorrow?"

"Yep, just have to go back to the doctor's office to have the burns redressed in two days."

Just then a very pretty nurse popped her head into the room. "Just checking to see if you needed anything before I get off shift."

Barrett lifted his head. "Are you leaving? I'm out of here tomorrow."

The nurse's face dropped with disappointment. She stepped into the room. Barrett shot us a *it was great to see you but get out* look.

I stood. "Call me tomorrow when you're ready to leave."

"You bet." He looked over at Taylor and winked. "See you later, Sis."

"Yeah, that's what I need— another brother." She leaned over and kissed his forehead and we left my brother behind with his extremely attentive nurse.

Chapter 24

Clutch

Lately it seemed to be the natural order of things in my life. Something fucking awesome would happen only to be followed by an explosion of shit. As promised, Aimee's father took care of Barrett's medical expenses, and he'd sent several affluent new clients our way. The Shelby was gone but business was booming. Taylor and I had been inseparable, and I spent every spare moment of my day thinking about her. Whatever her parents thought, she'd known all along that we were meant to be together, and while it had taken longer for the inevitability of *us* to penetrate my thick skull, I'd come to realize that there was no one else but Taylor. The only major flaw in all of it was that her family, including Jason, had no idea we'd been seeing each other. Not that I gave a damn what any of them thought anymore, but it was just easier, for now, to keep it quiet.

I just hadn't realized how much easier.

Jason walked into the office. His mouth was pulled tight in anger.

I leaned back in my chair. "What's up?"

He didn't say a word as he walked over to the small couch and sat down. His nostrils widened, and he seemed to be trying to control a fit of rage.

"Is there a problem?" I asked.

"I don't know, *Buddy*, is there?"

"Spit it the fuck out, Jason. I'm busy."

"Apparently, my mom was cleaning up Taylor's junk-yard of a room, and she came across a sweatshirt that was balled up and thrown in a corner."

I'd hoped his tirade would have nothing to do with Taylor, but obviously, it was all about to hit the fan. But I kept up my guard. "Well, that's just fucking amazing, Jason. Good for her. Now let me get back to work." I turned back to my computer.

"It smelled like smoke."

I stared down at the keyboard and thought about the things that had gone through my head to prepare me for this conversation. I spun back around and faced him. "That's because Taylor was with me the night of the fire. But I guess you and your awesome detective powers already figured that out."

He stood abruptly but I stayed seated. Jason was always intimidated by my size, and I didn't need that edge today. I knew I was on the right side of all of this.

"I love Taylor."

"She's not for you," he snarled. "I've already told you my parents don't want—"

"I don't give a fuck about them. She's eighteen. She can make her own decisions. If your parents are stupid enough to lose their daughter over their petty ignorance then that's the way this will go."

The side of his jaw twitched angrily. "Fine, but are you ready to end this partnership over it?"

It was a chunk of ammunition I hadn't expected. "Do

you mean that your parents still have so much control over your life that you would put your livelihood on the line just to please them? What the hell has happened to you? And why are you so against me in this?"

"I wouldn't be giving up my livelihood. I'll take my clients and you take yours."

"And we compete with each other in the same town? That's the stupidest thing I've ever heard. This business is booming. You really want to give that up just because I love your sister?"

"Just think about what I said." He turned to leave.

"So, I'm supposed to choose between business with you and life with your sister." He walked out of the office. "That's an easy fucking decision," I yelled after him.

I slouched back against the chair. It had happened again— a dramatic shift in my day. My computer dinged as another order came in. I stared at the monitor. For a while, there seemed no limit to what we could accomplish with this business, but now Jason was willing to throw it away. His loyalty to his parents and his bizarre need to protect his sister's virtue was going to bring it all to a halt. But I didn't need to give it a thought. I wanted Taylor, above anything else in this world, I wanted her.

With the shitty morning I'd just gone through, I worried what might be awaiting Taylor at home. I knew she was at school and wouldn't be able to answer her phone. I dialed her number and it went straight to voice mail.

"Call me. We need to talk."

Another call came in as I hung up. "Hey, Nix."

"You don't sound great. What's wrong?" Nix had the uncanny ability to read people's thoughts through the phone.

"What's right?" I asked.

"You need a night out. Dray is in a competition tonight and I told him we'd go. He's been in a bad way. Cassie got an offer for an overseas photographic journalist internship. She's thinking of taking it, and he's really down about it."

"I don't blame him," I said. There was a long pause, and it seemed we were both thinking the same thing. "Hell, when did women become the most important part of our lives?"

"I know. Who'd have thought? What do you say about tonight? Just a lot of beer and head busting."

"I'm there. I need a good dose of both."

CHAPTER 25

Taylor

My phone had died halfway through the morning, and I stared at it in my palm as I walked home. The entire day I'd had a creepy, tingling sensation on the back of my neck, and the dark, lifeless screen on my phone had been giving off bad mojo. I rounded the corner to my house and tried to drive off the uneasiness but then my feet froze. My dad's car was in the driveway. My dad was the type of man who never left work early or took off for a sick day.

I walked in through the side door hoping to slide through to my room without notice. The laundry room smelled like fresh soap, and my sweatshirt was hanging on the line to dry. I stopped and turned to look back at it, and my heart dropped into my stomach.

They were sitting at the kitchen table with mugs of coffee clutched tightly in their hands. The look on my mom's face said it all. They knew everything. I took a deep breath. Maybe this would be my chance to lay everything out. I opened my mouth to speak, but my dad held up his hand to stop me.

"Not a word, Taylor. We'll do the talking. Sit down here and listen." His icy tone sent a shudder through me.

I pulled out a chair and sat.

"Eighteen or not, you are under our roof." It was going

to be the *our roof, our rules* lecture. "Your mother and I have agreed that we need to do more to secure your future. You've blown any chance for a four year school with your failing grades and lack of ambition, but we're willing to pay for you to go to fashion design school."

"But?"

"But what?" Mom asked.

"But there is a catch, right?"

"No catch. You just have to promise to work hard because it costs a lot of money." Dad took a long sip of coffee, and I waited for the bomb to drop. "And, of course, you have to stop seeing Jimmy."

The chair scraped my mom's immaculate tile floor as I stood. "No deal. I'll figure out my own way to pay for it."

"We're not done talking," Dad said sharply.

"Then talk to each other." I reached the door just as his chair slid back. He grabbed hold of my arm and spun me around. "We've already taken care of things with Jimmy. It's over. You two won't be seeing each other anymore."

Panic set in and I looked over at my mom. She'd turned her gaze down to her coffee cup. I'd always been told I had my dad's eyes but, at the moment, his had flames in them. "What do you mean you took care of things with Jimmy?"

He released his grip on me. "Jason told him that the business partnership would end if he continued to see you."

"And Clutch agreed?" I asked making every attempt to stay calm. The last thing I wanted to do was lose it in front of them and give them any sense of victory.

My dad averted his eyes.

"Did he agree?" I asked.

"Jimmy is a business man," Dad said, "He's not going to give up everything he's worked for just for a fling with a pretty school girl."

"A fling?" The tears I'd held back broke through. "Is that really what you think this is? You haven't answered me. Did Clutch agree to Jason's terms?" My voice sounded shrill now, and I would have been pissed at myself if it hadn't felt as if every piece of me was crumbling.

There was no answer. I raced from the kitchen and slammed my bedroom door shut behind me. I stuck my phone on the charger. There was one voicemail form Clutch. My fingers trembled as I dialed up my voicemail, terrified about the message he'd left. It was brief. He wanted to talk. His voice was distant. Not like he'd sounded in the last few days, those few days when we'd been dizzy with each other's company. Or at least I had been. Maybe for him it had been just as my dad had so cruelly put it— a fling.

I curled up on my bed and cried. I didn't have the courage to call him back. I laid there staring at the room through blurry eyes. My mom had straightened it out, no doubt because it'd given her an excuse to snoop. She'd even straightened my sketching supplies. This time my carelessness had been my undoing. I'd taken off the smoke soaked sweatshirt and dropped it in a corner of the room. Because of the Shelby, they'd known about the fire at Clutch's house. But none of it mattered now if Clutch had just as easily given up on us to save his business.

Complete and utter despair pushed me into a deep sleep, and when I woke, my room was striped in the shadows of dusk. My head hurt and my throat was dry. I got up and walked into my bathroom for a drink of water and an aspirin. A knock startled me out of my drowsy state.

"Taylor, dinner is on the table." Mom's voice had the usual everything is fine pitch.

"Not hungry," I called from the bathroom.

Her footsteps retreated down the hallway. I swallowed two aspirin and trudged back to my bed. I glanced at my phone and was relieved to see that no one had called. I couldn't talk to him yet. I wasn't ready to deal with his excuses. I wasn't ready to face the reality of my heartbreak. I badly needed to talk to someone though, and lately, Scotlyn had been my one true friend.

I dialed her and she picked up right away. "Hey, Taylor."

I broke into tears at the sound of her voice and wanted to kick myself for it. "What's wrong, Sweetie?"

"My parents are demons, and my brother told Clutch that he would break up the business if he continued seeing me. He's worked hard for that business. Why would my parents be so stupid? Now I'm going to lose him for good." The last words came out on a series of sobs.

"I think you're completely wrong about that, Taylor. I know Jason and Clutch aren't speaking at the moment. You can cut the tension in the office with a knife, but Clutch is crazy about you. He's not going to give you up."

"My parents said he has already chosen the business over me." Just saying it produced an ache deep in my chest. Of course, he'd keep the business. I was just a silly nuisance to him.

"Look, Cassie and I are just finishing dinner."

"My gosh, I'm sorry. I didn't mean to interrupt your evening."

"No, Taylor, that's not why I brought it up. We've made a decision. It's probably a really stupid one, but Cassie's had a few pina coladas and she's decided we should go to the fights. Dray is competing. Nix and Clutch will be there. Come with us and then you can talk to him yourself."

"I'm afraid to talk to him. What if it's all true? I don't think I'm ready to face it yet."

"Taylor, get dressed. We'll swing by and pick you up in twenty minutes. Can you get away?"

I thought about it. The agony of not knowing was probably worse than knowing. "There's a little park two blocks before my house. Pick me up there. See you in a few."

Long ago, I'd perfected an escape plan, and I used it whenever my parents were pissed enough to forbid me from leaving the house. I turned on the shower to give the impression that their little girl was getting ready for bed. I tiptoed around and pulled on my jeans and a long-sleeve shirt. Then I brushed my hair up into a ponytail and turned off the shower. I flipped on the television and pulled on my boots. The screen in the window next to my bed had been pried out of its notches. I slid open the window, pushed open the bottom of the screen, and climbed out. After the drama scene in the kitchen, they would most likely check in on me later, but I really didn't care anymore. They'd been instrumental in destroying my happiness and ripping my heart to shreds. There just wasn't anything else they could do to ruin my life.

Cool air drifted up from the city below as I race walked to the park. My resolve to see Clutch had strengthened during the execution of my escape plan. In my rush to get out quickly and quietly, I'd left my cell phone behind on the charger. I stood under the giant oak at the corner edge of the park and waited. The quaint little park had become my clandestine meeting place, and if it hadn't been so awful knowing how often I'd had to sneak around, it would have been humorous.

Scotlyn's car turned the corner and pulled into the tiny parking lot. I climbed into the backseat.

Cassie peered over the front seat at me. "Hey, Taylor. Thanks for coming along on our ridiculous adventure. The more the merrier." She sounded nothing like the Cassie I knew. It was obviously the drinks talking.

"Sure thing. You know I'm always up for anything. Where are we going to watch Dray?"

Scotlyn glanced up in the rearview mirror at me. "Tank's Gym, and I have to admit I'm a little nervous about driving through the city."

"Do you want me to drive?" Cassie asked.

Scotlyn laughed. "No, I think we'll choose my inexperience behind the wheel over your rum soaked reflexes."

"Probably a good idea," I piped up from the backseat.

Scotlyn's blue eyes met mine in the mirror again. "Did you hear that Cassie was offered a photo journalist internship with a big international newspaper?"

"Whoa, Cassie, that's awesome. When do you start?"

Cassie fell silent for a moment. "I don't." Her uncharacteristically, happy-go-lucky tone had soured. "It would require me to spend six months traveling abroad." She glanced back at me. "I can't leave Dray for that long." Her face brightened again as she forced a smile. "He can't even feed himself properly." She looked over at Scotlyn. "Did I tell you what he made himself for dinner the other night when I had to work late at Freefall?"

"That good, huh?" Scotlyn asked.

"He made himself a French fry sandwich but there was no bread involved. He cooked two frozen pizzas and a bag of frozen curly fries, which he sandwiched between the two pizzas. He was so proud of his culinary feat, he wrote down the recipe so he wouldn't forget it." She shook her head. "It was a pretty simple recipe. Cook two pizzas and squeeze some fries between them. I told him it was just like one of those heirloom family recipes that we could someday pass down to our grandchildren." She sighed but some of the disappointment had returned. "Seriously, he doesn't even know how to replace the toilet paper on the holder. If he ran out he'd probably just start using newspaper. He'd never survive without me."

"Maybe you'll find an internship closer to home," I suggested.

She shrank down some in the front seat. "Yeah, maybe." she said quietly. I knew Cassie was crazy about Dray, but she was also crazy about photography. And she was extremely talented. It had to have been a heart wrenching decision.

Scotlyn gripped the steering wheel tightly as we pulled off the freeway and into the heart of the city.

Cassie brought up Tank's Gym on her phone. "Turn left at the light."

"Have you ever seen one of Dray's fights?" I asked.

"Only ones outside of the ring. It's probably really stupid of me to do this, but I figure, what the heck. Who knows— it might even be fun. Right?"

"Sure," Scotlyn said weakly.

I had no response. In fact, a hesitant hush fell over the car as we all seemed to be imagining the possible scenarios we might be met with in the middle of Tank's Gym. I had even more to worry about. I had no idea what to expect from Clutch. My earlier trepidation had returned.

"What's the worst that could happen?" Scotlyn broke the contemplative silence. "If we don't like it, we'll just turn around and leave."

Cassie nodded. "Just put in an appearance, eh? Good plan, Scottie." She looked out the window. "Jeez, this really is the seedy part of town."

I peered out at the scenery. An old guy was holding a conversation with a trash can or at least he seemed to be talking to it. "No, I think we passed seedy back when that guy was peeing on the bus stop sign. I think we're entering the bowels of the city now."

Cassie ran her thumb across her phone. "Oh, wait, turn right. It's just around the corner."

"I have to warn you that if parallel parking is required then we're turning back around and heading home," Scotlyn said.

Cassie pointed ahead. "Look, I think that one is big enough to pull into."

Scotlyn parked and once again an anxious silence fell over the car.

"The place looks dark," I said.

"I think the windows are covered with some kind of dark material. It's hard to see through the all the bars." Cassie looked over at both of us. "Why would you need security bars on a gym? I mean are people going to break in and carry off those big, unwieldy punching bags?" She sighed. "Let's go before my buzz wears off and I chicken out."

We climbed out cautiously as if we were stepping onto the surface of the moon or some strange planet. And in a way, we were.

Scotlyn looked back at her car. "I sure hope it's still here when we come back out."

Cassie pushed on the big metal door, and it creaked open. Instantly, our senses were assaulted with the sounds and smells of men. A heavy set guy with a frosty white goatee stepped in front of us. He had a wad of cash in his chunky fist. The entry way was dimly lit, and the row of spectators lining the ring in the center of the gym blocked any light from coming through.

The guy squinted down at us, and two chipped front teeth emerged from his smile. "Well, normally I'd ask ya' for fifteen bucks each, but we could use some sparkle in there." He motioned for us to go inside.

Instinctively, we all placed hands over our faces to block the stench of sweat. The timing of our arrival was perfect. The crowd, mostly guys, was so absorbed with the action in the ring, that nobody took notice of us as we scooted through the place. I stretched up tall and looked for the blond head that always towered over everyone else, but I couldn't find it. It was entirely possible that Clutch wasn't even in the place. I was slightly comforted by the idea that I wouldn't have to see him tonight. My stomach churned with worry, and now, more than ever, this really seemed like a stupid idea.

Self-preservation and the sticky cloud of unpleasant man smells sent us to the back of the gym where the only visible part of the fight was the spray of sweat when a fighter got slammed. Loud roars echoed off the cement walls of the building, and the dense air closed in on us. The din of the crowd made it impossible to speak to each other, but the looks we shot each other said it all. We should never have come. Some stuff was better left to the imagination.

Even though we couldn't see a thing, Cassie flinched every time the sound of knuckles smacking flesh shot up from the ring. Cheers thundered through the building, and the ground beneath our feet trembled. The fight in the center ring was over. Cassie's shoulders relaxed as both competitors walked out on their own and not on a stretcher.

Their attention no longer drawn to the ring, the spectators began to take notice of the three of us as if a spotlight had turned on above us.

Scotlyn took hold of my hand. She looked over at Cassie. "We should probably find the guys soon."

"Agreed," Cassie said. But, suddenly, we were like cornered prey in a den of predators, and with each cautious step we took, the predators moved closer. "All right," Cassie said. "I'm officially calling this a mistake." Then a side door opened on the opposite side of the gym and, aside from a few stragglers, the pack of hunters turned their attention back to the ring.

I stretched up on my toes in an attempt to peer over the sea of heads. One head stood above the rest. I took a sharp breath and dropped back to my heels. "I think Dray might be next in the ring. Clutch is one of the people who just came out of that side door. I can't see Nix and Dray, but I'm sure they have to be nearby."

Cassie took hold of Scotlyn's arm. "I've changed my mind. I can't watch this. I don't know what I was thinking. Let's get out of here."

"You only have to ask me once. It's probably best if we can scurry out of here without the guys seeing us." Scotlyn squeezed my hand even tighter, and I took hold of Cassie's hand. Scotlyn's long silver blonde ponytail lit the way as she pulled us quickly through the mass of testosterone. Through the maze of men, we spotted a clear but narrow path to the door. The rumblings and voices grew louder and the spectators pressed closer to the center ring. In seconds, our escape route had filled with men. I pointed toward an opening, and Scotlyn dove through it. Our quick and slightly frantic rush seemed to be drawing attention toward us again.

Without warning, a man's arm snaked around Cassie's waist. She lost her grip on my hand, and I pounded my fists on the guy's back. The stale smell of alcohol floated out of his mouth as he laughed at my futile attempt to harm him. Cassie grabbed his thick wrist and tried to pry his hands off of her.

Scotlyn pushed her face up into his. "Let her go, you creep." When she was pissed, she had some solid tone behind her usually demure voice.

Unfortunately, Scotlyn's scolding only served to draw more attention to us. Then moments later, the trip to Tank's Gym grew from a bad decision to a colossal, irreparable mistake. It was hard to know exactly when the impact had occurred. It had all happened so incredibly fast. Dray had shot across the room almost as if he'd had the preternatural speed of a vampire. He was standing between Cassie and the guy who had grabbed her. The nauseating sound of a nose breaking snapped through the low roar of the crowd and the guy stumbled back, blood pouring from his face. In a blur of movement, two large guys with tight black t-shirts that read 'security' shoved into the center of the action and dragged Dray roughly to the backroom. In the chaos of it all, I'd lost sight of Nix and Clutch.

Cassie's narrow shoulders shook with sobs. Scotlyn grabbed hold of each of our arms. "We've got to get out of here now." We inched closer to the ring where it seemed we could find our surest way out. Cassie kept her face down, and Scotlyn forged ahead with steely determination. We emerged from the sea of bodies and ended up directly next to the ring.

We crept along its border. We were halfway down the ring and just twenty steps from the exit when an announcer came on the microphone. "We are looking for a match up in round three. A fighter has been disqualified for throwing a punch outside of the ring."

Cassie's face shot up. Her glasses were steamed from tears and the moist, hot air in the gym. She pulled them off. "Did they say he was disqualified?"

Scotlyn looked at me and then reluctantly turned to Cassie. "I'm pretty sure that's what the announcer said."

Cassie's hand flew to her mouth. "Dray's been anticipating and preparing for this match for weeks. He's going to be so upset. I can't leave until I know he's all right." Her voice trembled.

Simultaneously, we glanced in the direction that security had taken Dray. The path to the rear of the gym looked daunting.

Cassie took a deep breath. She wiped her glasses off on her shirt and placed them back on her face. This time Cassie took charge, and with elbows swinging and expressions that told people to get hell out of the way, we made the long trek to the backroom door.

Something told me that Dray was not going to be in the greatest of moods when he saw us, but Cassie knew him better than me and she headed toward him now with unflappable determination.

Cassie glanced fleetingly at us before opening the door. A cold, dark corridor wound around a corner. Light and voices streamed out into the otherwise unlit passage. We followed the sound of the deep voices and came to another metal door.

Cassie's confidence seemed to shrink with each step we took. She pressed her hand against her stomach. "I feel sick."

Scotlyn placed a hand on her shoulder. "Maybe they won't suspend him for the whole night."

Yellowish light seeped beneath the door making Cassie's face look even paler. "I caused all of this." She opened the door and three familiar faces popped up. They stared at the three of us as if we'd just emerged from a spaceship. I didn't look directly at Clutch, but I could feel his gaze on the side of my face.

Dray shot Cassie a hard look. His jaw twitched as he spun around and paced toward the back wall lined with a row of dented lockers. He threw his fist into one, and the clang of metal echoed off the cement walls.

Cassie looked extra small in the vast room. She wrung her hands together with worry, and I walked over and put an arm around her shoulder.

Dray was the first one to find his tongue. "Have you three girls lost your mind coming down here? What the hell, Cass? Do you know how long I've been training for this fight?"

Cassie's throat moved as she swallowed. Her eyes looked glassy with tears, but she held them back. "I- I didn't tell you to hit the guy." Her thin tone was nearly lost in the stark tile and cement room.

"I can't fucking believe you girls came down here," Dray growled. "Fucking stupid stunt."

Cassie turned around and flew out of the room. Scotlyn followed her.

I looked at Dray. "She just wanted to see one of your fights, you ass—"

"Stay out of it, Taylor," Clutch said tersely.

Up until that point, I'd made little eye contact with him, but I made plenty of it now. There was a tiny flicker of regret in his eyes but not nearly enough to wipe away his admonishment. "Go to hell, Clutch."

"Taylor, dammit, come back here," he yelled, as I slammed the door and raced out.

I plunged through the crowd, ignoring the creepy comments and gestures. Cassie and Scotlyn were already at the car as I shoved open the metal exit door and stumbled out onto the grimy sidewalk. We climbed inside.

Cassie covered her face and slumped down in the front

seat as Scotlyn started the car. I glanced back. Nix and Clutch emerged from the gym and watched us pull away.

My stomach knotted up with pain as I thought back to the last few minutes. Clutch's cold greeting for me only solidified my hunch that my parents had been telling the truth. He wasn't going to give up his business for a silly, meaningless relationship with me. I felt hopeless and ridiculously delusional. For a brief amount of time, I thought I'd finally gotten him to take notice of me. For a brief amount of time, I'd convinced myself that Clutch wanted me as much as I wanted him.

Cassie sat up and pulled out her phone. She furiously typed out a text message and pressed send.

Scotlyn watched her and then looked up in the mirror at me. "Are you all right, Taylor?" I was glad they'd both missed my scolding.

"I'm just great."

"Me too," Cassie said sharply.

Scotlyn glanced over at her. "Did you send him a well-deserved, nasty message?"

Cassie shook her head. "Nope. I wasn't texting him. I just sent a message to the man who offered me the internship overseas. I've accepted the position. Dray just made the decision really easy for me."

"Are you sure you shouldn't wait until you're not angry at Dray?" Scotlyn asked. "It's a big decision to make when you're upset."

Cassie didn't answer her. She turned around and looked at me. "Taylor, you're still young. You make sure that you pick the future you want. Don't let any guy take control of your life. You too, Scottie. As awesome as Nix is, you've got to set your own future." With that, she reached forward, turned up the music, and slumped back against the seat.

We drove back in silence with only the memory of the horrid night to fill our thoughts.

I leaned over and hugged them both as Scotlyn dropped me off at my street corner. The front room light was on, but my bedroom was dark, giving me hope that they had never checked on me. I stared at the quiet house for a minute and realized I wasn't ready to go inside yet.

It felt as if I'd been knocked senseless like a fighter in the ring. My limbs felt rubbery and useless. I sat down on the curb in front of my house. Still being spring, the night time temperature was chilly enough to make me fold my arms around myself. Then I thought about being in Clutch's arms. I'd been in pure bliss for a few days thinking maybe things were going to go the way I'd wanted. I'd wasted so much emotion and heartbreak on the man and all for nothing. Cassie had been right. I needed to take care of my own future, and I needed to stop wasting time pining over Clutch.

Car lights swung around the corner, and I figured Scotlyn had decided to make sure I'd gotten inside. I pushed to my feet and squinted into the light, but it wasn't Scotlyn's car. It was an old beat-up car that I'd never seen before. The car pulled over to the curb in front of my house. I turned to hurry inside.

I heard a window roll down. "Taylor," a voice said.

I stopped and looked back. Gus's face peered up at me as he leaned over the passenger seat. "I tried to call you."

"I don't have my phone." My heart was still racing.

"You scared me. What are you doing here?"

He looked up at me. "You look like you've had a bad night."

"One of the worst."

"I'm sorry to hear that. I'm leaving in the morning." He stared up at me. "You should come with me."

Chapter 26

Clutch

Normally, I was one of those lucky people who enjoyed going to work since it was my own business and I was doing exactly what I loved to do. But I would have preferred to stay in bed today. After a quick and disappointing fight night, I'd driven Dray home. I'd gotten home and finished enough beer to knock out an elephant, or me, and then fallen into bed. I had hoped to drown out my own miserable thoughts with alcohol but realized there just wasn't enough beer in the house for that. Especially when the scent of Taylor's perfume still clung to my sheets and the pair of earrings she'd taken out still sat on my nightstand. I tried all night to call her, but she never answered.

The shop was empty as I arrived. I was just as glad not to see Jason. I had no idea how this was all going to end, but I knew that no matter what happened, I wasn't giving Taylor up. Now I had to worry that she'd given up on me. She'd left so pissed, I wasn't convinced that she'd ever talk to me again.

I filled the coffee pot and headed to my computer. There were orders waiting to be filled. Aimee's dad had given the shop a big boost with leads. She'd moved back home, and Dustin had disappeared completely. I could only hope he was living in a refrigerator box somewhere in the city.

The back door opened and shut. "Scotlyn?" I needed to

find out what'd happened after the girls left the fight. I only hoped she would tell me.

The footsteps were heavy, not Scotlyn's. Jason burst into the office, and I sat forward.

"Where the hell is she?" His fists were curled tightly.

"Who?"

"Don't fucking play games with me, Clutch. Where is Taylor?"

"I haven't seen her since last night." I pulled out my phone. "She was with Scotlyn and Cassie last night. I'm sure she stayed out on the boat." I dialed Scotlyn's number.

"Hello."

"Hey, Scottie. Is Taylor with you?"

There was a pause. "No, I dropped her off on the corner of her street. She wouldn't let me drop her in front of her house because she didn't want her parents to see that she'd gone out. Do you mean she didn't get home?" There was an edge of panic in her voice.

"I'm sure she just ended up at a friend's," I said calmly, even though I wasn't. "See you in a few, and don't worry."

I hung up. "Maybe she spent the night with a friend. Did you call her school?"

Jason's face was in its usual twisted state of rage, a look that he'd perfected lately but one that'd never suited him. "Of course we did. What do you think we are, idiots?"

I stood and he stepped back. "Yes, as a matter of fact that's exactly what I think of you and your parents. And, once I find Taylor, which I will, she's mine, and if you can't handle that then we'll talk about breaking up this business.

While your expertise with cars is valuable to me, my business sense is of way more value to you. You'll be shit out of luck without me, but I'll do just fine." I stormed past him and headed back out to my truck.

I'd marched out of the shop with all the confidence of a skilled tracker only to realize that I was completely unsure of where to start looking. I knew Taylor had a couple of friends she was close to, but they would be at school. I headed home. Barrett was closer in age and knew more of her friends.

***

Barrett was still fast asleep. The burns on his back were healing, but there was no way he could work. I kicked the side of his mattress, and he lifted his head and squinted into the daylight. "What the hell, Jimmy? What time is it?"

"It's ten o'clock. Sorry to wake you so close to the crack of dawn, but Taylor's missing."

His head flopped back on the pillow. "I don't think you need to worry. After all, it's Taylor. It's not like she hasn't disappeared before."

I yanked the sheets off of him and dropped them in a pile on the floor. "Get up. I need your help to find her. At the moment, she's really pissed at me." I walked out.

"So what? She's always pissed at you," Barrett called out. "Where the hell are my sheets?"

I checked my phone on the way to the coffee pot. There was a text from Scotlyn.

"Any word from Taylor?"

"Not yet." I wrote. "I'll let you know as soon as I hear

from her." There were no other messages or texts. I knew that Taylor's parents had taken her phone once as a punishment, but this time I was pretty sure she was just making a point of not answering my texts.

I poured a cup of coffee. I heard Barrett walk into the kitchen and turned around. "Want a cup?"

The look on his face told me he hadn't followed me into the kitchen for coffee. "What's wrong?"

His phone sat perched on his palm. He glanced at it before looking at me again. "I know where Taylor is."

"Where is she?"

"Alaska."

I placed the cup down hard on the counter, and hot coffee splashed my hand. "What are you saying? She left with that stoner?"

"Gus just texted me. They landed in Alaska an hour ago. He said Taylor was upset, and he invited her to move up there." Barrett's face mirrored how I felt, as if someone had just handed me a lit stick of dynamite. "Sorry, Jimmy. She's gone."

My phone buzzed and I looked at it. "Fucking hell, Dray's fight fiasco just started an avalanche of shit. Nix just texted me that Cassie's leaving Dray for a photography internship." I yanked out a chair and sat down. My limbs and head were suddenly filled with lead. "I've been a fool thinking Taylor and I were going to work all this out. She hopped on a plane with hardly a thought toward me."

Barrett sat down across from me. "Really? That's what you think? And I'm the idiot?"

I glared at him, but it didn't serve its purpose. He continued.

"You have been the only guy in that girl's whole damn world. There were plenty of guys after her in school, but she had this crazy notion that she was going to end up with you. I've never seen you happier, by the way, than these last few weeks. You're not your usual asshole self."

"Thanks."

"Any time. You said she was pissed at you last night. Well, then flying off to Alaska sounds exactly like something Taylor would pull. Cute as she is, she never thinks things out— like her crush on you. She should have thought long and hard on that. Cause like I said— you're kind of an asshole."

I sat forward fast enough to make my brother flinch. But I wasn't pissed at him. I was pissed at myself. The truth was, I'd thought of nothing else except Taylor since— since forever.

I pulled my phone out of my pocket.

"Are you going to tell Jason?" Barrett asked.

I shook my head. "First, I'm booking a flight to Alaska. Then I'll let Jason know we found her, but that's all I'm going to tell him."

"Awesome." Barrett slapped the table. "We're going to go fetch Tater Tot."

I looked questioningly up at him. "We?"

He stood up. "Uh, you may know just about everything, but you don't know your way around Alaska, or where Gus lives— Juneau, not Anchorage. You probably won't be able to book a direct flight this late."

"Can we rent a car in Anchorage and drive to Juneau?"

"Not unless the car has a bow and stern. There are no roads to Juneau." He turned to leave and then stopped. "Oh, and pack a coat. It's cold as fuck up there."

CHAPTER 27

Clutch

"Jeez, will you relax," Barrett said, "I could bounce a bowling ball off the tension surrounding you."

I tapped the pen on the counter. "This isn't tension. This is full blown anxiety." I looked over at my brother. "What if we find her and she tells me to go to hell?"

"Then we turn around and head back to California."

"That wasn't the response I was hoping for. I thought you'd tell me that she would never tell me to go to hell."

The guy returned with the keys, and I pushed the rental contract across the counter to him. We were the only customers in the place, but it had taken him a good forty minutes to finally get to the point of handing us the keys. He took some glasses out of his pocket and stuck them on to look over the contract. I figured it would be another fifteen minutes before we left the place. His finger slid over the paper and then he stopped and glanced up at me over his spectacles. "You're from California?"

"Yeah, is that a problem?"

He shook his head. "Not at all. If you're looking for work up here, I know a few fishing boat captains who'd take you on for sure." He returned to the contract. "Well, everything looks good. Do you need a map? The roads out here can get pretty tricky. It's easy to get lost."

Barrett pointed to his head. "I'm his map. We'll be fine."

"Are you all right with a manual transmission? I've only got a jeep left."

"His nickname is Clutch."

That humored the man. "I guess that means manual will work for you."

I took the keys in my hand.

"Right out that door and to the right. Can't miss it."

We left the counter. I glanced over at Barrett. "Yeah, why the hell should I be anxious? The woman I love will probably hate me even more for following her here that is if we can even find her so that she can break my heart face to face. And, now we're in the middle of nowhere, surrounded by glacial mountains, and I've got you for a map. Why the hell should I be worried? Sounds like an awesome time all around."

We walked outside, and the wind cut us like sharp blades of ice. I shoved my hands into the pockets of my coat and scrunched my face down below my collar.

"Told you to bring gloves," Barrett said.

"I can't believe people actually live here."

"You're just extra wimpy because you're from the land of bright sun and blistering heat waves. Believe it or not, since it's spring, this is actually balmy. In January, you'd be taking your balls off and sticking them in those coat pockets."

The jeep looked as shabby as the tiny car rental office we'd just come from. We climbed inside.

"I hope the heater works," Barrett said.

"If it doesn't then I'm sitting on my hands and driving with my knee." A few turns of the key produced a rattling engine. We pulled out onto a long, two lane highway. A half mile down the road, the heat kicked in. "The scenery looks like it jumped out of a painting."

Barrett stared out the window. "It's pretty fucking awesome up here." He looked down at his gloved hands. "If I hadn't fucked up like I always do, I'd still be up here."

"From what you've told me, it was your buddy, Gus, who fucked up." My jaw clenched as I said the guy's name. Barrett seemed to sense my sudden change of mood. "Just thinking about that guy putting his hands on her—"

"Stop thinking about that, Jimmy. She told me they were just friends. Besides, we're not in Los Angeles anymore. These guys up here are tough as leather and they stick together. You can't take this out on Gus. It's not like he kidnapped Taylor. She packed her bags and left voluntarily with him."

"Yeah," I twisted my hands around the steering wheel. "But I still want to kill him."

Barrett leaned forward and pointed through the front windshield. "Check that out. I'll bet you've never seen that before."

I leaned down and peered up. A huge eagle with a wingspan as wide as the jeep glided above the road and then disappeared into a copse of evergreens. "That was cool. Hell of a lot bigger than I would have expected."

"They grow everything bigger up here. You should fit right in. The grizzly bears up here make the California black bears look like toys. There are wolves too. In fact, there's a whole pack of them that live up near Gus's cab

. . ." He glanced over at me. "I guess you probably didn't want to know that."

"Probably not."

"There's a motel off the road over here. It has a diner. Let's check in and go eat something."

"I don't want to waste any time. It already took longer than I thought to get here." "You've got to be kidding? That girl has been chasing you for two years. I think you can wait a few hours before you start chasing her back. She's only been here for a day."

"I'm not chasing her." The statement sounded even more stupid aloud than it had in my head. "I'm tracking her."

Barrett laughed hard enough to steam up the window. He fiddled with the defrost button, but it only made things worse.

"Christ, Rett, I can't see a fucking thing."

He reached forward with his gloved hands and smeared the condensation across the windshield.

"Gee, that helped a lot."

"That's all right." He pointed to the left side of the road. "There's the motel and the diner. The office closes at dark. If we don't check in we'll have to freeze our asses out here in this jeep all night."

"Fine, but you aren't much of a tracker. I doubt Daniel Boone stopped to check into a motel when he was out forging trails."

"I doubt he forged trails in a jeep either."

We threw our duffle bags onto the beds in the tiny, dark motel room and headed across the parking lot to the diner.

I stuck my hands back in my pockets and averted my eyes from the icy air. There were only two other trucks in the lot besides the jeep. "After leaving Los Angeles where each of us has only a few square feet to ourselves, this place is almost creepy it's so desolate. It's like we landed on Venus or something."

"Neptune," Barrett corrected me. "Venus is one of the hot inner planets. Neptune is a cold one."

I glanced over at him. "Impressive. You must have paid attention in class occasionally."

"Only in third grade science when we studied the solar system. It's the only topic that caught my attention. We had to make solar system models at home."

"Oh yeah, you used Mom's fruit because she wouldn't buy you Styrofoam balls."

"Everyone else showed up with these fancy elaborate models to share, and I had to carry in my piece of cardboard with fruit glued to it. Saturn, the grapefruit, kept falling off because it was too heavy. Then I got a D because at the last minute Mom yanked off Earth, the apple, and stuck it in my lunch, glue and all." He shook his head. "No wonder none of us did great in school."

"Mom and Dad were great at providing the survival basics, but they seemed to think that was all we needed."

We stepped inside and a gruff looking man greeted us. "Sit anywhere."

There were six round tables and only one was occupied by two men. They stared openly at us as we walked to a table and sat down. One spoke up immediately.

"Looking for logging work?" he asked, directing his

question at me.

"Uh, no, just here for a visit."

"Too bad." He went back to his meal.

Barrett smiled as he stared down at his menu.

"What's so funny?" I asked. "And, why the heck is everyone offering me jobs up here?"

He looked up at me. "Well, Paul Bunyan, why do you think? You look like you could throw a lobster pot over the side of a boat with your bare hands and push down a tree with a kick of your boot."

I picked up my menu and leaned back against the chair. "Well, if I'm Paul Bunyan then you must be *Babe*, my blue ox."

The same gruff looking guy with a prickly, gray beard and deep wrinkles came up to take our order. He looked down at me over his writing pad. "I heard Becker hired a new timber faller. You must be him, huh?"

Barrett's shoulders shook with a silent laugh, and I kicked him under the table. "Nope, just in town to visit."

"My mistake. You look like a logger."

I glanced at the menu. "I'll have a double order of meatloaf and potatoes."

He grinned. "Certainly. We call that the lumberjack."

"Of course you do."

Barrett handed him the menu with an annoying grin. "I'll have the single order."

I leaned forward. "How far is Gus's place from here?"

"He lives in a kind of remote area. I think it's about an

hour from here."

I glanced out the wavy glass window at the front of the diner. "Do you mean there are places even more remote than this?"

"Yep. We're lucky it's spring though. There will be more hours of daylight. I don't think I could find my way to his place in the dark." His mouth drew tight, and a rarely seen, serious expression crossed his face. "What are you going to do when you get there? Gus isn't exactly a lay down kind of dude. He'll be pissed when we show up."

"Shit, Rett, you act like I'm going to just tear into his house and rip the guy to shreds."

His brow lifted. "Don't tell me that scenario hasn't crossed your mind a few times."

"A few times, yeah. But that's just what I fantasize about doing. I'm just going to go up there and ask to talk to Taylor." I looked out at the empty land that seemed to stretch on forever. "Taylor loves adventure and anything dangerous, but there's no way this place would keep her entertained. Or maybe that's just wishful thinking on my part." I looked at my brother. "I still can't believe she just took off like that. I thought I meant more to her than that." The old guy lowered two plates of food in front of me, and I stared down at them. As hungry as I was, nothing looked appetizing. My stomach was knotted with nerves. There was a real possibility that I'd lost Taylor for good, and that thought had ripped a bottomless hole in my chest.

Barrett reached for the ketchup bottle. "You do matter to her, but everyone has their limits. You never told me why she was so pissed at you."

"I don't know. The whole thing was such a blur. I was

still reeling with rage at Jason for handing me an ultimatum between business with him or Taylor. Then I went to Dray's fight with Nix. And for some reason, the girls showed up at Tank's Gym."

He nearly choked on a piece of meatloaf. "By girls, you mean *The Girls*?"

"Yep, Scotlyn, Cassie and Taylor. I have no idea what prompted it, but there they were, looking as out of place as three delicate daisies in a sea of brambles. Dray had no idea they'd come to watch. Unfortunately, he saw a guy grab Cassie and he decked the guy. Tank disqualified him and he never got to the ring."

Barrett noticed that I was only picking at my food and aimed his fork at my second piece of meatloaf.

"Go ahead. I guess I don't have a lumberjack's appetite, after all."

He doused the second piece with ketchup and carved it with his fork. "That doesn't explain why Taylor was pissed at you."

"Things just rolled downhill fast. Nix and I took Dray into the back room. I've never seen him so pissed. Cassie and the girls came into check on him, and he yelled at Cassie. She stormed off. Taylor turned on Dray for being such a douche, but I stopped her and told her to stay out of it."

Barrett stared at me in slight disbelief. "You told Taylor to mind her own business?"

"Not in so many words, but. …"

He shoved a piece of meatloaf onto his fork. "You're going to be in the doghouse a long time for that little misstep."

"Yeah, I guess. But running off to Alaska was a bit of an overreaction."

He swallowed a big mouthful and drank down some water. "Piece of advice, Bro, keep that obvious observation to yourself. It won't help your case when you're talking her into coming back with you."

CHAPTER 28

Clutch

"I think I've seen more trees in this one afternoon than I've seen in my entire life put together."

Barrett had taken the wheel. He'd claimed it would be easier for him to find his way back to Gus's if he was driving, and I was glad to let him. It gave me an opportunity to look at the scenery and think about what I was going to say to Taylor once I'd found her. The whole thing was pretty damn ironic. She'd chased me around for two years and now I was chasing her. But, never once did I question whether or not I should have been in Alaska. I had to find her. If she didn't want to come back with me then I would have to deal with that shitty reality, but I had to know for sure.

A thick layer of dark clouds capped the icy peaks surrounding the town. I tried to coax the heater to produce more warmth, but the rusty, old jeep was giving all that it had. I rubbed my hands together and blew into them. "It's official. I'm a California wimp. This place is beautiful, but it's too damn cold. Give me seventy degree Christmas mornings any time."

"You get used to it eventually. But I can tell you that December and January were a true test of manhood, especially out on the Bering Sea. I would have cried if I hadn't been worried that my tears would freeze on my face. It was so fucking cold out there, my sinuses burned with frost bite. The wind chill out there was so harsh, if a wave washed over you it would feel like bath water compared to the air. One time I hit my hand hard on the sorting table, and I was sure the thing was going to just snap off." He turned the jeep up a long narrow road. We headed up into the mountains. The higher we drove, the more patches of snow we saw.

I peered up through the cloudy windshield. "Those clouds look menacing. Will it snow?"

"Nah, it's too warm for that. Probably just rain, really cold rain." He stopped in the road and threw the jeep into reverse. "I think I missed the turn off." He backed up directly down the middle of the road. "Here's something you don't get to do in L.A."

I smiled. "You could do it, but you'd probably get shot by the other drivers."

He made a sharp right turn onto an unpaved road. "Yeah, this is it." He pointed through the windshield. "The pine tree that looks like it has two heads is my marker. Lightning strike, according to Gus." He glanced over at me. "His cabin is just up the road."

It was all I needed to hear. My heart was beating hard against my ribs. I still hadn't formulated what I would say to her. Something told me that even if I had a script printed in my head, all of it would float away the second I saw her. Taylor had that kind of effect on me. She'd always had that kind of effect on me. I'd just denied it for far too long.

The sky above darkened with heavy storm clouds, and yellow lights glowed in the few cabins we passed. Thin streams of smoke swirled up from stone and brick chimneys. Barrett turned up onto a steeply pitched path. The jeep chugged up the hill and then a small, rustic cabin came into view. The cabin was surrounded by towering pines, and the roof looked as if it sagged beneath the weight of dried pine needles. Logs of wood were piled high and long enough to cover the entire side wall of the house. Otherwise, the place looked sad and lonely as if no one had ever lived there.

"It looks dark, like no one's home." Just thinking about Taylor living in the shabby, unfriendly cabin sent a chill through me.

Barrett parked the jeep, and we climbed out. The small window in the front door was crusted with dirt. We walked up the creaky front steps and I knocked. There was no answer or movement inside.

"Are you sure you've got the right place?"

"I've been here a bunch of times." Barrett looked at his phone. "No reception up here. I can't text him. He'd be pissed anyhow." He hopped down from the porch and walked around back to a small garage. He smeared the dirt off a small side window and peered inside. "Gus's truck isn't here. He hangs out down on the pier at a bar. It's not that far. Let's go down there and see if anyone has seen him."

"Them," I said. "Remember, Taylor's with him." It was hard to believe, but I was actually hoping she was right there by his side. Then I would at least know that she was safe. The empty cabin had left me with an icy knot in my gut, and now I was even more anxious to find her. I needed to know she was all right.

We climbed back into the jeep and coasted down to the

road. Sprinkles fell on the windshield, and Barrett searched for the wiper switch. They worked about as well as the jeep's heater, and we both instinctively leaned forward to get a better view of the road.

"We really only have to worry about wild animals running into the road," Barrett said cheerily.

"Could you please stop talking about wild animals. As it is, my stomach is twisting around that chunk of meatloaf."

"Don't worry, Taylor can take care of herself."

"Yeah, when she's in her sunshiney, suburban neighborhood where there are no grizzlies, wolves or blizzards."

"It's spring. I don't think blizzards are a problem. Unfortunately, grizzly mamas and their cubs are just starting to wake up from their long winter naps."

I stared over at him, and he quickly remembered my request to stop talking about wild animals.

We drove another half hour. Juneau was nestled tightly between mountains, and even though it was not a large town, it seemed like it took forever to get from one place to another. My worry grew with each long, cold mile of wet road. The defroster in the jeep was a joke, and with my nerves on edge, I was glad Barrett was behind the wheel.

A deep blue bay of water came into view as we drove around the curve of the main road. Barrett didn't dare take his hands off the wheel, but he motioned to the left with his chin. "If you look through the haze, you can see a small pier behind all the anchored boats. That's where we're heading."

"I just hope we find them there. Something about that deserted dark cabin has my stomach in a knot. I've got a really bad feeling about all this."

"We'll find her. Don't worry." Barrett turned down a short road that ended right where the pier started. He turned off the engine and looked at me. "If he is here with her, he'll be surrounded by all his buddies."

"And, you're telling me this why?"

"Just keep a lid on the temper, big brother, or we'll both end up strapped to the bow of a ship."

"I just want to see Taylor and know that she's all right." We climbed out. "And I don't have a bad temper."

Barrett found an annoying amount of amusement from that declaration. The temperature had dropped profoundly since we'd first stepped off the plane at the airport. Out on the water, it was, as Barrett had warned, cold as fuck. The rain had stopped once we'd reached sea level, but the clouds still hugged the mountain tops assuring us that rain was falling at the higher elevations.

The moored boats bobbed up and down in the dark, choppy water. Loud voices rumbled out of an open doorway. Barrett stepped into the place first. Glowing lights on the walls made the place far more inviting than the inside of the jeep. A few heads turned as we entered. One man looked me up and down and opened his mouth to say something.

"I'm not looking for work," I said.

"Too bad." He returned his attention to his plate of food.

"Hey, Barrett," the bartender called across the room, and a few more heads turned.

I scanned the room for Taylor but couldn't find her or Gus for that matter. It seemed we'd reached another dead end.

"Hey, George, have you seen Gus?" Barrett asked as he approached the counter.

George looked puzzled and then he motioned with his head. "He's right there at the end of the bar."

Gus was draped over a large glass and pitcher of beer, hardly aware of anything going on around him. Taylor was nowhere in sight. I was overwhelmed with worry, and before Barrett could stop me, I stormed over to him and shook his arm to get his attention. I'd gotten everyone else's attention too.

Gus nearly slipped back off his stool as he lifted his face high enough to see me. The guy was as drunk as anyone could be before collapsing into a worthless heap. His lids drifted down as if keeping his eyes open was a chore. He noticed Barrett for the first time and smiled. "Hey Barrett," his words were slurred, "what brings you to town? If you're looking for that crazy bitch, she's gone."

I grabbed hold of his shirt and several chairs scooted across the floor. Barrett put a hand on my arm. "He can't tell us where she is if you knock him senseless."

I released him.

"Where did she go?" Barrett asked. He glanced back at the angry scowls that circled us. "Everything is fine. We're just looking for someone." The scowls remained. They closed in on us, but, at this point, I was ready to take them all out with one fist.

Gus looked up at us again as if he'd forgotten we were standing there. "That chick is as crazy as they come. We'd barely landed at the airport when she was begging me to send her home. I wasn't about to spend more money on a ticket back to California. She already owes me for the first ticket."

My jaw was clenched tightly, but I managed to spit coherent words out. "Where is she now?"

The scumbag just shrugged and lifted his beer glass to his mouth. I smacked it out of his hand and it went flying into the mirror over the bar. The glass and mirror shattered, and more chairs scraped the floor. Gus stood up quickly and then stumbled back a few steps before grabbing hold of the bar to steady himself. I could feel the heat of the men behind us as they moved closer.

Focusing on me wasn't easy but Gus managed it. "I have no idea where that bitch went, and I hope I never see her again."

Barrett knew me well enough to place a restraining hand on my arm, an arm that was ready to throw a fist into the guy's face. "Let's go, Jimmy, she's obviously not here." He leaned closer and lowered his voice. "And you won't be able to find her if you've been pummeled into a pulp by Gus's pals. We're outnumbered big time."

In another twist of irony, Barrett was being the voice of reason. I nodded and fished out my wallet. I tossed a hundred dollar bill onto the counter and looked at the bartender. "For the mirror." Then I pulled out two more bills and shoved them into Gus's pitcher of beer. "For her plane ticket."

Gus lifted his head. "If the cold hasn't gotten her already then there are plenty of hungry wolves scouring the woods."

I turned. We'd almost made it out, but the asshole's last comment was too much. My elbow shot back and made direct contact with his face. He flew backward off the stool.

His loyal security guards didn't move. Barrett and I stood in the center with fists tightened and ready to defend ourselves.

The tension in the surrounding circle melted, and one guy walked over to help Gus to his feet. Another one shrugged. "After that last comment he deserved it. I hope you find the girl." He looked out the window. The water was angrier and the sky was black with storm clouds. "And soon."

We got into the jeep as if we had some plan, some fucking clue where to go. Raindrops pelted the windshield and seemed to freeze up in crystal shaped ice pellets the second they hit the freezing glass. Barrett turned on the engine to get some heat flowing out of the dash. Our breath came out in short, cloudy bursts. The black feeling I'd had in my gut earlier had grown, and a sense of complete helplessness washed over me.

With no other idea what to do, I sent her a text message knowing full well that there would be no response. I stared at my phone hoping I could magically draw out an answer, that she would tell me she was safe. I texted Scotlyn and Jason to see if they'd heard from her but neither text went through. "I don't even have any bars on my phone. We're in the middle of the fucking North Pole up here."

Barrett pulled the jeep back onto the road.

"What the hell are we going to do, Rett? Do you know where the police station is? Maybe she ended up there."

"That's where I thought we'd start. Try not to freak out yet because you are the guy who always keeps his cool and his head. If you lose it, then I'll lose it right behind you."

I shook my head. "There's no way I can keep my head when it has to do with Taylor. She has been the biggest thorn in my side for two years." I stared out at the lethal looking storm clouds. With every minute of daylight disappearing, the rain came down harder and colder. I thought about Taylor out there somewhere all alone. "If anyone ever pulls that thorn from my side, I will bleed to death. Shit, Rett, I need her. I can't even think about life without her."

"No kidding. I was wondering when she'd finally penetrate through that iron skull of yours."

The jeep's windows frosted up, and it seemed there would be no relief from the defroster in the dash. I reached forward and wiped off the condensation with the edge of my coat sleeve, but I only made things worse.

"Great," Barrett quipped. "I used to at least be able to see where the road ends and people's yards begin."

"Sorry. How much farther is the station?" Taking charge of stuff was always easy for me. My confidence had always led me successfully out the other end, and it was rare for me to feel despair but I was definitely feeling it. Dozens of horrid scenarios danced around my head, and I could not rid myself of them.

"It's still a few miles."

"She has no money, and worse, she probably doesn't have much more that a sweatshirt to keep warm. It seems colder than even the coldest winter night in California. There was no way she was prepared for this physically. I can barely stand it myself."

"It's a small enough town that someone somewhere had to have seen an unfamiliar, pretty girl dressed in ridiculously light clothing," Barrett said. "We'll find her. She can't have gotten far."

Visibility seemed to decrease around every corner, and Barrett had to slow the jeep. My body was rigid with tension. I knew if he went any faster we risked hitting something, but it still didn't decrease my urge to slide my leg over to the gas pedal and step on it.

We entered the downtown area, which, aside from the tall, tree covered mountains looming above the city, looked like any other small town with shops and buildings lining a two way main street. Being closer to civilization and the conveniences of a city, no matter how small, made me feel better. If Taylor had just managed to get to Juneau, she would have been able to find help.

Not surprisingly, the Juneau Police Station was quiet and calm. The officer at the front desk looked up as we walked in. "Is there a problem down at the lumber yard?" he asked.

"Don't know anything about the lumber yard." I pulled out my phone and thumbed through my pictures. Taylor smiled up at me from the screen, and I showed it to the officer. "We're looking for this girl."

He looked at the picture a few seconds then handed the phone back to me. "How old is she?"

"Eighteen. She flew up here with someone, and now he doesn't know where she is. She's from California. She's probably underdressed, and she has no money or phone."

"She's an adult."

"Believe me, no one is more aware of that than me. Can't you put out a bulletin or whatever it is you send out to the squad cars so they can keep an eye out for her?"

He looked at Barrett and then at me with a touch of suspicion. He seemed to be assessing whether or not all of this was legit. "What's your name?"

"James Mason. We're from California."

"You mentioned that. Do you have some identification?

I yanked out my wallet and pulled out my license. He looked it over and handed it back to me.

"Do you have a picture besides the one on your phone?"

"No, just the phone, but I can give you a description."

He sighed as if he was not pleased to have to attend to any actual police business. He reached into his drawer and pulled out a pad of paper in slow motion. I clenched my fists to keep from pounding the counter to speed him along.

"You said she's an eighteen-year-old female?"

Barrett sensed my angry tension and placed a hand on my arm to warn me to stay cool. "Yes. She is about five-foot-eight with long, copper colored hair."

The officer's brow lifted and he looked up at me. "Copper? Like a penny?"

"Yeah, I guess."

"How much does she weigh?"

"I don't know that."

He peered up at me over the counter. "You don't know?"

I looked pointedly down at his wedding band. "When was the last time you asked your wife how much she weighed?"

"Good point." He returned his attention to his pad of paper just as a door opened from the back room.

Another officer walked out. "Hey, Henry, I'm going out to old man Cooper's place."

The guy looked up from his pad of paper, and my fists clenched tightly again. This had been a mistake. We would have been able to cover more ground without the police.

"Why are you going out there?"

"His neighbor, Penelope, called. She said Cooper's got his shotgun pointed at that old shed of his. Thinks he's cornered a bear or wolf inside, but Penelope was sure she could hear a girl crying."

"This is Mr. Mason and he's looking for a lost girl." The officer behind the counter looked up at me. "Follow Officer Tucker. Sounds like we found her." He looked at his fellow officer. "You'd better hurry. You know that senile, old man can't see past his nose. And he loves to point that gun at anything that moves."

Every muscle in my body tensed. "We'll be right behind you. Is it far?"

Officer Tucker was already at the door. "It's just around the corner, but we need to hurry. It only takes a second to fire off a shotgun."

I drove, thinking we'd be flying through the wet streets like race car drivers. I was wrong. Officer Tucker's definition of *hurry* was to go five miles over the speed limit. He even stopped at the light.

"This can't be fucking happening." My frozen fingers gripped the steering wheel like steel vices. "He hasn't even put on his lights or siren. I could have followed him on foot and kept up."

"This isn't Los Angeles. Life moves much slower and stress free out here."

"Stress free? There's nothing stress free out here if they

allow half-blind old guys to have shotguns."

"Everyone has a gun out here. It's like living in the wilderness."

We turned the corner along a narrow road with no paved sidewalks or streetlights. The sun had gone down, and the layer of clouds made it one of the darkest nights I'd ever seen. We pulled up in front of a house with a porch light that blinked on and off like a strobe. It was hard to make out much, but there was a small white shack adjacent to the house.

Moving with the speed of a sloth, Officer Tucker climbed out of the car, and Barrett and I were right behind him. A small, unsteady figure stood in the shadows of the house wearing a yellow rain slicker and holding a gun that was far too heavy.

Tucker lifted a hand to stop us. "We don't want to startle him. He's pretty out of it, but at least it looks like he has fired his gun yet." Tucker looked at me. "And with his eyesight, he might just mistake you for a grizzly."

"Mr. Cooper, it's Officer Tucker."

It took a long, torturous moment for the old man to respond. He turned and stared at Officer Tucker, but he didn't lower the gun. With no city sounds and tree covered mountains to absorb any noise, it seemed as if someone had put the whole world on mute. And then, through the stillness, a small, helpless sound drifted out from the shed, and my heart broke with the sound of it. Loaded shotgun or not, I had no more patience for slow motion. At the risk of being gunned down as a grizzly bear, I pushed past Officer Tucker and the barrel of the gun. Before the officer could open his mouth to stop me, I yanked open the door of the shed, nearly pulling it off its hinges.

It was pitch black and freezing cold inside the shed. Junk was piled and cluttered along the walls. The soft sobs had stopped, and I could hear shallow breathing.

"Taylor," I called into the darkness.

A beam of light came through the doorway from Officer Tucker's flashlight. She stepped out of the shadows and relief surged through me. Her face was pale and tear-streaked, and her lips were nearly blue from the cold. She had only a hooded sweatshirt for warmth, and it was soaking wet. A heavy backpack hung from her fingers. Her lips parted and it seemed to take all of her energy to speak. "Is it really you or am I unconscious and dreaming this?"

I closed the gap between us with two steps and pulled her against me. She trembled almost uncontrollably, and her knees weakened. I slid the backpack onto my forearm and swept her up into my arms. Officer Tucker led us back to the jeep with his flashlight. "Do you all have a place to stay tonight?"

"We're out at the motel on the highway," Barrett answered.

"Get her there quickly and into a hot shower."

I lowered Taylor into the backseat and climbed in next to her. Barrett fired up the engine and cranked the heat as high as it would go. I unzipped her sweatshirt and pushed it off her shoulders. She was wearing only a thin shirt beneath. I took off my coat and wrapped it around her. She laughed weakly as it engulfed her completely. I pulled her, giant coat and all, into my lap and wrapped my arms around her.

She lowered her head to my shoulder. "You came for

me." Her wavering voice drifted up from the thick folds of my coat.

"Of course. You belong with me, Taylor, and don't ever scare me like that again." I tightened my arms around her.

"I always knew nothing bad could happen to me in these arms," she said softly. Her words went straight into my chest.

CHAPTER 29

Taylor

Both of my parents' cars were in the driveway. I squeezed Clutch's arm nervously. "They are going to kill me or send me off to a convent. I'd prefer the first option."

Clutch hadn't said much the entire ride over from his house, which didn't help the insane flurry of butterflies in my stomach. We climbed out of the truck, and he took my hand as I walked around to the sidewalk. He pulled me toward him and his free hand pressed against my face. My throat tightened as my gaze met his. I'd always been head over heels for him, but now my emotions for him ran so deep, I could hardly breathe when I was near him.

He leaned down and kissed me. "I love you, Taylor Flinn." Then he took hold of my hand and we walked to the front door. My parents met us in the entryway. My mom gasped in relief and broke into sobs when she saw me. Dad was equally relieved, but he played it much cooler.

"Thank goodness, you're all right, Taylor," he said sternly, leaving no doubt that I would soon be in for a major lecture and whatever other fun they had in store for me. Dad looked at Clutch. "Thank you for bringing her home." There was a dismissive tone to his thank you, and I was about to say something but Clutch spoke up first.

"Mr. and Mrs. Flinn, you've known me for a long time.

Jason and I have a good partnership, but to please you, he has threatened to break up the business if I don't stop seeing Taylor." He paused. "That's never going to happen. I'm going to date Taylor. I waited until she was eighteen. I make good money. I'm a decent person." He looked at me. "I won't give her up. So, if that means the business is finished then so be it. Jason needs me a lot more than I need him. I need Taylor a lot more than I need any of it. She wants to go to art school and learn fashion design, and I'm going to pay for her to go. So, you can learn to accept that we are together and still have your amazing, incredible daughter in your life, or you can lose her forever because I'm not giving her up."

A hush fell over the entryway, and I thought I could almost hear my dad's pulse pounding through his veins. And then he looked over at my mom and silently they seemed to come to an agreement. Dad stepped forward and shook Clutch's hand. I walked over and put my arms around my mom, and we both cried as we hugged for the first time in years.

I walked Clutch out to his truck. He leaned against it and dragged me against him. I peered up at him. "That was a good speech."

"I felt like one of those guys from the eighteenth century having to ask for permission to court the king's daughter."

I hopped up on my tiptoes and kissed his chin. "Do you think the Vikings had to ask permission to court their ladies?"

He smiled down at me. "Nah, I think they just took women whenever they wanted them."

"Really?" I wriggled suggestively against his hard body.

"No wonder I have a thing for them."

"Yep, that's what they do." He lifted me on to my toes and kissed me lightly. "And the wilder the woman, the better."

"Perfect." My arms went around his neck and I kissed him.

2637

32870495R00168

Made in the USA
Lexington, KY
05 June 2014